Satan's Gun

Nineteen year old Sam Bryson faces a conflict that will test his courage, character and faith. Sam had been raised by his grandparents since he was three years old. He had been given his first pistol on his thirteenth birthday and ordered by his grandpa to practise every day, except Sunday.

Albert Bryson's dilemma is that his beloved wife had brought Sam up to reject violence, leaving him vulnerable in a cruel and violent land. He orders Sam and his cousin, Jack, to hunt down Sharkey Kelsall who is wanted for murdering a Bryson ranch hand and whoever gets Kelsall will inherit the ranch.

Sam Bryson has no reason to fear any man nor any desire to kill, but he will soon discover that his life is threatened by others and that he must protect himself.

Satan's Gun

BILL WILLIAMS

A Black Horse Western

ROBERT HALE · LONDON

ISBN 978-0-7090-8316-0

Robert Hale Limited
Clerkenwell House
Clerkenwell Green
London EC1R 0HT

Typeset by
Derek Doyle & Associates, Shaw Heath
Printed and bound in Great Britain by
Antony Rowe Limited, Wiltshire

With thanks to my wife, Dawn, family and friends for their support and encouragement and to Mark Bannerman for his help and advice.

ONE

I'd ridden into Klanbala Town just a few hours ago hoping to find Sharkey Kelsall who I had been trailing for weeks. I hadn't expected to be joining a party organized by the marshal and be here three miles out of town preparing to watch a grave being dug up in the darkness. I'm not sure that I liked Marshal Tom Daly very much, but he might be about to help me return home tomorrow without having been obliged to kill anyone. With luck I could stop looking over my shoulder in case I was being trailed, and being jumpy waiting for Kelsall to shoot me as I passed by some rocks or trees.

'Bring those lamps over here,' Daly barked at his deputies. The frown on his heavily lined face was fiercer than usual. The marshal was a powerfully built man of about forty and his thick greying hair stuck out from the sides of his tan-coloured leather Stetson. I'd heard that he'd lost his wife and two young daughters when his house was burned down in a revenge attack, so maybe he had some reason for being mean all the time.

'What did you say your name was, kid?' Daly shouted at me.

'Sam Bryson, sir,' I replied, giving him the respect he probably didn't deserve.

'And how old would you be, Sam Bryson? No more than sixteen judging by that girlie skin of yours.' Daly gave a weak smile as he winked in the direction of the deputies.

Deputy Carter didn't seem in the mood for jokes and muttered, 'This is crazy,' making sure that the marshal didn't hear him. Carter couldn't understand the desperate haste. He might have had a point, because it wasn't as though the body buried near the yew tree where Carter was now standing holding the lamp was likely to disappear. Unlike Carter, I was anxious to see if my search for Sharkey Kelsall was over. Daly didn't comment when I told him that I was nineteen because he was too busy pushing the prisoner he'd brought from the cell in town.

'Right, Grindley,' the marshal roared again, 'you miserable excuse for a human being! Start digging and don't try any funny business, otherwise I'll blow your head off and bury you where you drop.'

Joe Grindley picked up the shovel that the marshal had thrown at his feet and pushed it into

8

the soft soil. Grindley had the appearance of a corpse. His dark eyes were sunken in the gaunt face that was pale and pock-marked, his remaining baccy-stained teeth were set in dark red gums that frequently bled.

Deputy Carter looked sympathetic as he watched Grindley struggling to dig out the grave, but his buddy, Deputy Luke Myers was smiling, clearly enjoying the proceedings, until Marshal Daly ordered him to take over the digging.

'I didn't think grave-digging was part of my duties, Marshal,' Myers moaned, as he watched Grindley fall to his knees with exhaustion.

'I've just made it so and you'll thank me when you're having your supper later instead of your next meal being tomorrow's breakfast.'

Myers was a raw-boned man of twenty-two, with broad shoulders and forearms that were bigger than Grindley's upper arm muscles. Within five minutes he'd dug out two feet of earth. The smell must have hit his nostrils as the impact of the shovel sounded different. Marshal Daly caught the stench and told Myers to let Grindley take over again.

I'd offered to help with the digging, but the marshal said it wouldn't be appropriate because I wasn't authorized and reminded me that I was only there to identify the body.

Grindley stopped digging and began retching

when the naked body was visible. Marshal Daly pushed Grindley out of the way and beckoned me to come and take a look. Grindley had claimed he'd buried the man there just over a week ago after he'd found him dead. The insects and worms had been busy feasting on the decaying flesh. I had seen a dead person before but not with the eyes chewed out.

'Bryson, is that the man you've been after?' asked the marshal.

I had already decided that it wasn't Sharkey Kelsall on account of the dead man's hair being fair and Kelsall's was black. He'd fled from my grandpa's ranch just over a month ago after he'd shot dead Tommy Cooke during a card game. Tommy was only nineteen years old and we'd grown up together. Some folks had said that we could have passed as kin having the same blond hair and pale-blue eyes. That might be so except that I'm six foot two inches and Tommy had been no more than five foot seven which was something I used to tease him about.

'I don't know how you can be so sure, Bryson,' said the marshal, 'because there isn't much left of his face.' The marshal must have been disappointed that he might not be getting the reward I'd promised him if he helped me catch Kelsall, but he wasn't about to give up and ordered Myers to wipe away the soil and insects from the face.

When Myers refused, the marshal accused him of being a weak-livered excuse for a man and then told Grindley to do it. Grindley dropped to his knees once again and gingerly brushed some soil away.

'Get out of the way,' roared the marshal impatiently when Grindley began retching again. The marshal removed his neckerchief and then knelt on one knee before using it to wipe away the remaining soil and insects to reveal the grotesque features of the corpse.

'Well, well, Grindley. You're going to stand trial for murder because this poor soul died from a bullet in the head and a jury will have to decide whether it was you that fired it.'

As I studied the badly eaten face and the naked body I was suddenly struck with horror when I realized that I knew this man: it was my cousin Jack who had been hunting Sharkey Kelsall just like me.

I guess I need to explain a few things.

I'd spotted Kelsall's palomino tied to a hitch rail outside the marshal's office. There was no doubting it was his horse because it was branded. I'd just missed him at the last town I'd stopped at, but there was more to my hunting him than just because he'd killed my best buddy.

I was raised by my grandma and grandpa since I was three years old after my folks died of a fever. My dear old grandma passed away last year but

Grandpa Albert was still alive and kicking back in Chevin Falls. Grandpa had made it sound so simple when he'd explained what I had to do, but it wasn't. He didn't think I had it in me to run his ranch when he got too old or passed on. So he decided that me and my cousin Jack should hunt down Kelsall and bring him back to face the law, or kill him if we had to. It was to be a kind of test to decide which of his grandsons would run the ranch. Cousin Jack was seven years older than me, had gotten himself into enough fights in town and on the ranch so he didn't have to convince Grandpa on that score. I suspect that Grandpa knew that Jack wasn't too interested in taking charge and hoped that I would bring Kelsall back, or at least prove that I could look after myself. Because I was much younger than Jack I had been given a day's start on him.

I'd had no intention of killing anyone, but I might not have had any choice because according to the barman in the last town, just thirty miles from here, some unfriendly looking guy had been seeking me. It could have been Kelsall, but the description was too vague to be sure it was him.

After I'd spotted the palomino outside the marshal's office I had explained to him that I believed a wanted man was in town. I was a mite relieved when Marshal Daly told me that the feller who had ridden into town on the palomino was locked up in a cell. The man had been thrown in the cells because he'd got really drunk and hit one of the saloon girls who had rejected his attention. My relief soon turned to disappointment when I saw Grindley in the cell and not Sharkey Kelsall. It seemed that Grindley had also been flashing his money around and the marshal figured he'd robbed someone. Grindley had told him that he'd come across a dead man, so he'd buried him after he'd taken his money and his clothes and then made off on the palomino. None of this made sense unless Kelsall had killed Jack and then taken Jack's horse. Maybe Grindley was innocent, but how did he come to have the money?

Marshal Daly ordered his deputies to fill in the grave after he said that it wouldn't be right to disturb whoever it was and rebury him in the town's cemetery. I had the feeling that it was more to do with him not wanting to be bothered with the extra work than any concern he had for the dead man. If there was the slightest chance that it was Jack's body then I would make sure that he got a decent burial in the town's cemetery.

'Well, that's one hell of coincidence if that's your cousin,' the marshal snarled at me when I told him I thought it was Jack's body.

Marshal Daly ordered the men to stop digging and told them to strap the body to Grindley's horse, and he'd already made it clear to me that I would have to pay for Jack's burial.

The short ride back to town was covered mostly in silence apart from the occasional laughter from the two deputies and the odd moan from the marshal who was clearly upset at missing out on the reward. His mood eased when we reached town and I gave him fifty dollars for his trouble. He was even helpful when he hammered on the door of Henry Oxlade, the town's undertaker, and arranged for Jack's body to be prepared for burial in the morning.

Jack's funeral was a simple affair but I was grateful that Henry Oxlade had arranged for a few of the older townsfolk to attend and Marshal Daly had ordered his two deputies to join him.

Before the final spade of soil was spread on Jack's grave I was heading for town eager to prepare to continue my pursuit of Kelsall. Any doubts I had about killing him had gone. I would still try to capture him alive but now that it looked as though he must have killed Jack I wouldn't hesitate to shoot the no-good snake if I had to.

The marshal had told me that Henry Oxlade had examined Jack's body and it looked as though he had been shot in the back before he received a shot to the head. Before I left town I tried to convince the marshal that I believed Grindley was innocent, but the marshal still intended to put him on trial. The marshal could accept that Kelsall might have taken Jack's horse and left the palomino, but refused to believe he would have left the bundle of money behind for Grindley to pocket. Marshal Daly had no doubt that Grindley had killed Jack.

The marshal suggested that I went to Bothey Waters because it was the most likely place that Kelsall would have headed, if he was a gambling man. It was a big logging town with plenty of men trying to win enough money to have a lot of fun at the saloons, and that meant working their way through the girls.

As I rode out of town I was determined that wherever Kelsall was I would find him and make sure that one way or another his days of killing would be over.

TWO

I headed west knowing that the scenery could only get better and within a couple of hours' ride I was entering what turned out to be just about the most awesome terrain I had ever seen with some magnificent stretches of water. I wasn't really a fishing man, but I couldn't resist having a go in that clear rippling water and giving Motty a chance to rest. I'd only had the grey gelding a few weeks and he was nothing special. I didn't expect Grandpa would be too pleased when I told him that I'd lost one of his best horses at a card game and ended up with Motty. The feller who sold him to me tried to explain how he got the name Motty, but I was suffering with a bad head at the time on account of not being used to drinking so much so I didn't understand the explanation. I just remember that it wasn't exactly because it was anything flattering.

Grandpa had tried to get me interested in fishing when I was a boy because we lived near the River Arupen, but I just didn't take to it.

I'd had the feller in the diner back in Klanbala Town make me some grub and I'd bought supplies at the store so I didn't really need to catch any fish to eat, but I just felt lucky. I always carried a bag with an assortment of useful items, well, mostly junk really, but sometimes I can produce just what I need. So I cut me a length from the ball of string and selected a medium sized bent rusty nail from my collection. I hacked me a branch off a nearby tree and trimmed away the side shoots. Grandpa reckoned that the most important thing was the bait which needed to be smelly to bring the fish to the spot and then tempting enough for them to sample it. I couldn't ever remember if he used cheese, but it was all I had.

Judging by where the sun was it must have been pretty close to noon. I wouldn't have any trouble drying my clothes off so I waded in. I fancied a bit of action fishing, not the lazy lying on the bank sort, waiting for them to come to you.

I must have been in the same spot long enough to attract at least a little one so I guessed if this beautiful river actually had any fish then they weren't partial to my bait. My feet were beginning to tingle as the coldness of the water seeped through my boots so I decided to move further upstream to try and get into slightly deeper water.

17

I thought I'd tripped or slipped at first even though I'd heard the gunshot. Then I felt the pain in my left shoulder, but I couldn't see how much damage the bullet had done because I was on the move downstream. I remembered thinking that if the son of a bitch tried a second shot he would have to be good to hit me at this speed. I was beginning to take in large mouthfuls of water because for a boy who was raised near a river I'm ashamed to say that I'd never got the hang of swimming. I suspected that this river only allowed swimmers to go in one direction and I was heading that way without any effort on my part.

I was relieved when the current eased and I was able to steer myself towards the bank. But any thought that I would survive was forgotten as I was taken by surprise and thrown to the side. I heard the crack above the sound of the flowing river as my head struck against a rock.

THREE

I'm usually one of those folks who wake up slowly and I was in no real hurry to open my eyes, and this bed was sure comfortable. I like to dream a little, let the imagination run free for awhile. Think of pretty girls falling for me, fast-gun Sam. I started to think of being on a paddle steamer and playing at the gambling tables. That's when I thought of water and that's when I remembered being hurtled down that goddamn river. The throb from the back of my head reminded me that I'd struck my head against a rock. Yes, I remembered the rocks and I remembered being shot at. It was painful to open my eyes, not helped by the bright sun that was shining through the small window. I didn't know how I'd got here, but perhaps the old man who was in the next bed would tell me when he woke up.

I was wondering who had brought me out of the

river because I doubted if it was the old-timer. I guessed someone had kitted me out with some of his clothes though and the white night shirt reminded me of my grandpa. A peep inside the night shirt revealed a bandage on my upper arm that had streaks of red on it where the blood had seeped through. It didn't hurt much and I guess I'd been lucky. I would ponder later why I'd been shot and whether it was some no-good thief, but probably decide that it could only be Sharkey Kelsall, the man I hated.

I was considering giving my companion in the bed beside mine a good morning hello when I heard the latch and saw a woman enter the cabin. I smiled at her and was curious to know how I ended up here, and was eager for her to explain. She had a basket of food which I hoped was for me because my mouth tasted like a fish had died inside it. The woman must have been about thirty-five, with raven hair, and was wearing jeans and a blouse that showed off a truly womanly shape.

'Thank God, you're alive, mister. I didn't know whether I was going to find two bodies in here this morning.'

I let my eyes drift away from the bulges in her blouse to the bed beside me. I started to say, 'You mean he's—' but she interrupted me.

'I hope you didn't mind being alongside my husband's pa. Tobias died yesterday right in the middle of eating his dinner. It's a bit cramped in our little house, but we'll be burying him later so he'll be out of your way.'

'How long have I been here?' I asked, with my eyes still fixed on the corpse.

'It was late yesterday when my Hank pulled you out of the water. You seemed a bit rambling whenever I popped in last night, then you just fell asleep. I've put your dry clothes over there, but it's best that Hank doesn't know that I made you comfortable by putting that nightshirt on. He's a bit funny about that sort of thing.'

I could have sworn that I'd heard Tobias snoring earlier, but thought that I'd better not mention it to her.

Nancy introduced herself and explained that her husband Hank ran a small lumber business and was getting ready to send some logs downstream when he spotted me. She said that I would be pleased to know that whoever shot me hadn't stolen anything, as far as she knew, and my horse was safe. My thoughts turned to Sharkey Kelsall and I had mixed feelings about whether I wanted him to think I was dead. I might have more chance of capturing him if he came looking for me, but I hope it wasn't before I'd recovered.

I sat up ready to eat some of the food she'd brought me, but she insisted on feeding me, which meant she sat on the bed. I had never had a woman this close to me before, rubbing herself against me like this. When I lied and said that I wasn't feeling hungry she said that she'd make me some eggs and beans later. She also promised me something that I would never forget and laughed when she said it was her special bread.

Nancy stroked my arm and said, 'If you weren't such a big, strong boy you wouldn't have survived, and that would have been such a waste. Hank said the bullet just creased your arm so you really must be lucky as well as handsome. I've never seen such curls on a man.'

'It must be a bit lonely out here,' I said, and immediately regretted it.

'Some women wouldn't mind and I didn't at first, but I do miss the excitement of living in a town. Hank works hard, but I don't get to see him except at mealtimes and he's always so tired for other things when we bed down, but I don't expect you know what I mean by that.'

I thought it best to play the innocent, but she smiled and said, 'I think you do. You're blushing. That's real cute, honey.'

I mumbled something about being hot and she dropped the topic, but moved even closer to me so that we were now lying side by side and she was looking a bit flushed. She looked sad when she told me that she would miss Tobias, who wasn't a bit like his son. It seems that he was full of energy the night before he died. When she ended by saying that Tobias had been so virile for a man of his age I guess that explained why she was going to miss him.

I must have looked as embarrassed as hell when the door opened, but she was as cool as you like, acting as though it was perfectly normal to be lying next to a complete stranger.

'Hi, honey. I wasn't expecting you until later. I was just feeding this young hunk of man. He's still weak as a kitten.'

Hank looked a bit older than Nancy, a thickset man, with cold eyes. His tanned face seemed troubled; perhaps he was upset about his pa. He didn't say anything to me when I thanked him for saving my life, but told his wife that it was time to do the burial.

Hank lifted his pa off the bed and headed out of the open door. Nancy followed him, but not before she'd given me a wink and said that she hoped I wouldn't be lonely tonight.

I'm not experienced with women, but I wasn't that dumb not to know that Nancy had been coming on strong and that could only mean trouble. I didn't want to play around with another man's wife, especially when he had saved me from certain death. So much for the advice I'd been given by an old ranch hand that women needed to be 'warmed up' before they got interested in love making. He'd said that unless it was nature's time for them to mate they were like cold fish and only did it out of duty. Perhaps it was Nancy's time, but I had a feeling that it was always going to be that way for Nancy.

I was a bit woozy when I got out of bed, but by the time I'd dressed I was feeling better and made my way outside.

Motty was unsaddled and tied to the hitch rail in front of the main log cabin and I headed over to reacquaint myself with him. I was still stroking the horse some minutes later when Hank and Nancy came out of the house. Hank had changed into a black suit and he had replaced his woolly hat with a wide-brimmed black Stetson, which I guess was his Sunday best outfit. Nancy was now wearing a pink flowery blouse that was even more revealing than the other one. I told them that I was going for a walk to get some air, and Nancy advised me to be careful that I didn't overdo things. Hank remained silent and for some reason he scowled at me.

I was only a short distance from the house when I heard the swift flowing river below, but decided to stay on the higher ground. I didn't want to get lost, so didn't venture too far and seated myself on a fallen log and watched some tiny birds darting amongst the trees. I would give Hank and Nancy some privacy while they buried Tobias before I headed back. I fully intended to leave later today before I was left alone with Nancy again.

My legs felt weak when I returned to the cabin and I was thinking that perhaps I would stay another night and hope to keep Nancy at bay. Motty's snort had me looking in his direction and I was surprised to see that he was all saddled up. Hank was standing in the doorway. He'd changed back into his working clothes and he sure looked angry as he came down from the stoop with my clothes bundle and hurled it to the ground in front of me.

'You're not welcome here anymore, mister. I'm sorry that I didn't leave you floating in the river.'

I was about to ask why he was so riled with me when he saved me the trouble.

'I can't abide men who mess with another man's woman. I know some women are easy game, but luckily my Nancy isn't like that and she told me that you've been making advances towards her, and taking advantage of her caring nature.'

I was tempted to repay him the favour that I owed him by telling him that his Nancy was a no-good man-eater who had been sleeping with his late pa, but I didn't suppose it would do any good.

I tied the bundle to Motty's saddle cantle and mounted.

'I'm sorry about your pa, Hank,' was all I said before I rode away without seeing the scheming

Nancy. Perhaps she had tried to make him jealous or she wanted to pay me back for not responding to her advances.

I had always regarded women as gentle folk who had no malice, but it appeared that they had cunning ways that I hadn't realized.

I'd been looking forward to the meal that Nancy had promised me earlier and my unexpected departure had left my belly making strange sounds which I suppose was nature's way of telling me I needed some food. I had tried a bite on a sour apple that I picked from a tree on Hank's land, but I wasn't quite that desperate yet. If I followed the river for a couple of miles it should take me into Bothey Waters, the town where Hank sent his logs downstream and the place that Marshal Daly had suggested I might find Sharkey Kelsall.

I hadn't covered more than a half a mile when I heard my name being called. At least it wasn't Hank coming to settle a score after he'd brooded some on me lusting for his wife. In some ways it might have been less complicated if it had been. I must have gained some experience of women because I wasn't surprised when Nancy drew her small piebald mare alongside Motty and begged to come with me. She didn't care where I was heading. She said that she could never go back to Hank because he was insanely jealous and he'd hit her. When she showed me the bruise on her cheek I agreed to let her ride with me into Bothey Waters.

Nancy chattered almost non-stop during the first part of the journey, but she didn't try to proposition me again. I still sensed that she was giving me the eye, sort of studying me. I wondered if it was my arrival or the passing of Tobias that had made her want to leave Hank. I asked her if she ever wanted children, suggesting that it might have eased her loneliness.

'I'm not the mothering kind, honey,' she replied, 'which is just as well, because nature hasn't given me any so far. It hasn't been for the lack of trying, apart from my time with tired Hank.'

She went quiet after the talk about kids and I suspect that she liked the idea of having some more than she would admit.

FOUR

Nancy seemed to get excited when we reached the edge of town and, as we rode down Main Street, we seemed to attract too much attention for my liking. Nancy was no stranger to the place judging by the number of men who called out to her. Most of the remarks were crude, but Nancy obviously liked the attention she was getting.

'That's the best hotel in town,' Nancy said, pointing to the Dakota Hotel across the street, and then added that it was the only one. I hoped the inside was in better condition than the front entrance with its faded and peeling paint, not to mention rotten wood. I told her that I might not be able to stay in a hotel because my money was on the low side. The unexpected cost of burying Cousin Jack had been something that I hadn't bargained for.

'I've got enough money for both of us and it'll

be cheaper if we share a room,' Nancy suggested.

I got angry with her and told her again that I wasn't interested in her. I had important things to do and she would just get in the way. I was grateful for her looking after me, but that was all. I suggested that she might want to go back to Hank when she'd reflected some.

'I'm never going back to him,' she cried.

'Perhaps a night on your own might make you see things in a different way. If Hank was jealous then he must care for you.'

She didn't say anything so I dismounted and was helping Nancy down from her horse just as a big feller with a bushy beard headed in our direction. He sure looked mad and it soon became clear that I was the cause of his anger. But then he turned on Nancy.

'So you've taken to sleeping with boys now. You whoring bitch,' he roared.

'You need to watch your tongue, mister,' I said, much to my surprise, because I didn't fancy my chances brawling with this mountain of a man, even if he did look a bit long in the tooth. To make matters worse he was joined by what appeared to be two of his buddies and they weren't exactly midgets.

'Give the kid a good beating, Tug,' urged one of them.

- 'Yeah, mess up that pretty face of his. He's a no-good wife stealer,' said the other.

I was thinking that they must be buddies of Hank and I was preparing for the worst when Nancy spoke. 'Tug, honey, you ought to be grateful to this young feller for saving me from a beating when I told Hank that I'd made a terrible mistake and wanted to go back to you.'

Nancy pointed to the small bruise on her cheek to support the story that she had just made up.

Tug looked puzzled and was obviously mulling over what she had said, but at least he had calmed down for now. I was beginning to feel unsteady on my feet and had already decided that if the big ape or his buddies made a move on me then I would go for my gun.

'What makes you think that I'll take you back?' said Tug, without sounding too convincing.

'Because we were good together, honey, and you are my husband. I never would have left you if you hadn't been working all the time. You know I need a lot of attention. Anyway, I realized that you are more man than Hank will ever be, especially where it matters to a woman.'

'She's one horny bitch,' drooled one of the men in a low voice, which luckily for him Tug didn't hear; perhaps he was too busy staring at the buxom Nancy who was flaunting her body at him. She was also fluttering her eyelashes in that funny way that women sometimes do.

'Well maybe I was a bit neglectful, but I only worked hard so you could buy pretty things,' Tug said, clearly taken in by Nancy.

'I know, honey, I realize that now,' said Nancy, as she moved even closer to the big man.

One of Tug's buddies indicated to the other that it was time to leave, obviously sickened by the soppy talk and perhaps disappointed not to have seen some of my blood on the dusty street.

'Let's go home, honey. I'll come back for your horse later,' said Tug, his voice gentle and his face smiling.

Nancy linked with his arm and they walked off, but not before she had given me one of her come-on winks.

I led Motty across the street to the Dakota Hotel, hoping that I could afford to stay there. The inside was everything the outside wasn't. It was more like a hotel that I had seen back East with expensive-looking decorations, but I didn't take to the weasel-featured feller at the desk with the greased-down hair and thin moustache. He gave me a cheesy-smile welcome, and told me the nightly rate and the special price if I was staying for a week. I told him that it would just be for a couple of nights and he looked disappointed.

'Of course, your room price does include a few extras which I'm sure a young feller like you will approve of.'

'You mean a bed?' I said sarcastically, still shocked by the price.

'I see sir has a sense of humour,' he replied, and then explained that they operated a voucher system and handed me a slip of white paper.

'If you hand that in at Charlie Wong's diner down the street on this side, you'll get 10 per cent off any meal.'

I gave him one my meanest looks after he thought it was necessary to explain that it meant ten cents off every dollar I spent.

I picked up my key and prepared to head to my room when weasel man said that I had another voucher coming and he was sure that I would appreciate this one. He placed a box on the counter and asked me to pick out one of the small pieces of folded paper.

I asked what this was about and he said, 'All in good time.' So I picked out one and opened it to reveal a number eight, which is my lucky number. The little guy said, 'Let's hope you're lucky.' He ran his figure down the list that was on a large piece of paper he'd produced from under the reception area desk.

'Ruby,' he announced, 'not bad. I don't think you'll be disappointed.'

He showed me the list that contained girls' names and I saw the number eight alongside Ruby. He wrote 'Ruby' on the blue paper voucher and told me that I could have a half-price session with Ruby, who was one of the girls at Marley's saloon.

When I asked what the one star next to her name meant he looked a bit uncomfortable. I'd noticed that the other girls had at least three stars against their names and Betty Lou had five against hers.

'It's a sort of rating, but it's really down to a matter of taste. Ruby might have a low rating which I compile from comments made by my guests before they leave, but it doesn't mean that Ruby isn't a desirable woman. In fact I can tell you that one man always insists on asking for her when he visits the saloon, so you might have to wait until he's finished.'

I was tempted to leave the blue voucher on the desk, but picked it up and headed to my room, which turned out to be clean and comfortable. It was also very large and contained a big double bed which was welcome because of my size. The room faced on to the street; this probably meant that it wasn't worth turning in until the saloon had closed and the rowdy cowboys and loggers had left town.

I had a wash from the fancy bowl on the table in the corner of the room, changed my shirt and headed back out into Main Street. I was soon pushing open the door of Charlie Wong's diner, hoping it wasn't too pricey because I intended to have me one good-sized meal. The thought of this left me feeling a bit guilty because I hadn't settled Motty into the livery and I expect he was just as hungry as I was.

The jovial feller who owned the diner was an Irishman named Mick. He was the third Irishman that I'd become acquainted with and they'd all had the same name.

'Before you ask, young feller, the previous owner wasn't Charlie Wong. I just made the name up, figuring that folks would think that a Chinaman could rustle up more interesting and better grub than a paddy.'

I glanced at the price of the items on the board and they were so low that I ordered double eggs, beans and fried mashed potatoes.

Mick asked me if I was sure that I really wanted double and smiled when I said yes.

'As long as you know that I don't tolerate any waste in here. That's why I have that notice up the there.'

The notice read: *Eet all you orrder – or else.*

'I haven't eaten in a long time so I think I'll manage a clean plate,' I said, hoping that Mick was better at cooking than he was at spelling.

Mick advised me that I had been warned and disappeared out the back after he'd poured me a large coffee. I seemed to remember someone telling me that the Irish were good at singing, but judging by the noise coming from the kitchen I decided that Mick was a better speller than a singer.

'There you go. Enjoy it, cowboy,' Mick said with a smile.

The plate was about the same size as grandma used to use for our big Sunday dinners and the food was piled high, but I had no doubt that I wouldn't be upsetting Mick. I was having second thoughts when he appeared at my table later with another plate that was nearly half-full.

'Sorry about having to use two plates. I've got some larger ones on order from back East, but I don't know when they'll get here.'

I'd had no trouble demolishing the contents of the first plate and was halfway through the second when I discovered that each mouthful that I swallowed seemed to be having trouble finding a place in my belly. It didn't help that Mick was resting his chin on his hands, clearly enjoying watching me struggle. I swear that by the time there was just one egg left on the plate it looked more than double its actual size. I had several burps and retches before I swallowed the last morsel.

Mick clapped and whistled his appreciation and told me that I was one gutsy kid and should consider eating as part of a circus act. He was still smiling when I settled the bill and slowly made my way to the door. I didn't present him with the voucher and left him a tip. It was real good value because I didn't intend to eat again until next week. As I was leaving I asked Mick if he had ever heard the name of Sharkey Kelsall or anyone who fitted the description I gave him. I was getting used to people shaking their heads like Mick did, but he did say that if Kelsall was a gambler then he would end up in this town.

I managed to take Motty to the livery without being sick, but I led him there even though it was the other end of town. It wasn't out of kindness to Motty, but because I didn't fancy the struggle it would have been to get on his back. When I left the livery I headed further out of town to the logging port, hoping that I might see some notices advertising jobs, but I didn't. I lay down by the waters' edge and mused whether I'd been a fool to reject the attentions of Nancy. It wasn't long before the effects of my over-full belly had me dozing and it was going dark when the siren from a passing ferry boat woke me up. My mouth was dry, but at least I wasn't feeling sick any more, so I scooped some water from the river and splashed it on my face and then headed back to town.

I had planned to give Marley's Pleasure Saloon a miss, but when I reached The Silver Bucket I saw the *CLOSED FOR RENOFATION* sign and it had me thinking of Mick. So, I headed for Marley's. At least I might get to see Ruby, but unless I ended up drinking more than was good for me I didn't plan to use my voucher.

The saloon was crowded and my entrance went unnoticed, apart from the smile I got from one of the saloon girls. I ordered a beer and took a seat away from the card game that was going on. A dude was trying to play the piano, but nobody seemed interested, perhaps because he was so bad. Thanks to my grandma's perseverance I was quite a reasonable piano player, a fact that never did please Grandpa. Once I had my first pistol Grandpa made me practise target shooting and how to draw fast every day, except Sunday, but that was just to please my grandma. It was a short-barrel Peacemaker .45 and I'd used it for a couple of years. I'd added quite a few to my collection since then and I'd kept them all. Grandma had disapproved of guns, especially mine, and she often rowed with Grandpa about me neglecting my piano playing and school work, but Grandpa had always insisted that my gun practice came first. As far as he was concerned no one ever stopped themselves from being shot because they could play the piano or were educated.

I'd spent hours and hours in Colby's store during the weeks before my eighteenth birthday until I finally settled on the Remington Frontier .44 pistol that I had in my holster right now. The Remington Frontier .44 was not to everyone's liking and some men wouldn't have had one for free, but I wouldn't change mine for the most expensive gun money can buy. And that includes the latest Peacemaker and the Smith & Wesson Schofield that some folks rave about. I didn't take to the Frontier straight away, but the more I used it, the better it felt.

I remember the last conversation I had about guns with Grandma when I had returned from practising with my new Remington on my birthday. She had been sitting in her usual chair on the porch doing her knitting and she looked troubled as she invited me to sit by her. She told me that she would stop objecting to me wearing a gun, now that I was a full-grown man, but made me promise that my gun would never become a 'Satan's gun'. I asked her what she meant and she told me that it was a gun belonging to a man who enjoyed killing. She didn't like any form of killing and feared that one day I might misuse the skill that God had given and use my gun to kill for pleasure. She seemed pleased when I said that I didn't intend to kill anyone and my gun would never belong to Satan. She still intended to pray for me every day to make sure that evil temptations were kept at bay and she hoped that God would keep me safe. Grandpa used to shake his head and smile when she started preaching and lighting candles and he would sometimes say, 'As long as it keeps her happy'.

Grandpa had worked hard and fought for the ranch he had built up and told me that he had been forced to kill men to protect it and said that I might have to face the same prospect one day. He had told me more than once that the law couldn't always be relied upon. It might be different one day but there were times when a man had to do the protecting of his land and property himself. I would be reminded of what Grandpa had said about the limits of the law, but it wouldn't be for a long time.

I was finishing my second beer when Nancy's big ape of a husband came into the bar and appeared to be looking for someone. It must have been me, because he headed straight for my table. Some of the men looked scared as he passed them and some greeted him as though they were friends, but he didn't reply. I was thinking that Nancy might have landed me in trouble by telling him she had feelings for me, but she hadn't.

'Nancy said you're looking for work. Well, there's a job going at my logging yard if you don't mind long hours and hard work. Be at the yard by seven o'clock in the morning if you're interested. Just head for the river and ask someone to direct you to Tug's.' He turned away from my table without waiting for me to speak and left the saloon. I expected it was his way of thanking me for helping Nancy, not knowing that I hadn't.

I had wandered around the bar earlier, hoping I would spot Kelsall at one of the card tables. I asked the barman and a couple of young fellers without any luck. Maybe the weasel-faced man at the hotel was right that Kelsall might be using different names while he was travelling about, which was what most gamblers usually did.

I was on the point of leaving when two men came and sat at a nearby table.

My ears pricked up when one of the men said, 'It looks like Ruby is in for another quiet night.'

There was only one woman at the bar. She was wearing the kind of dress that showed most of her bare back. Judging by the looks of her skin she wasn't young, but she was certainly curvy. A cloud of smoke appeared above her head and I noticed the fancy cigarette holder she held in her long fingers.

'Ruby's in luck,' said one of the men, and nodded in the direction of the two men who were heading towards her. One of them was supporting the other, who was blind. I wasn't one for making fun at the unfortunate, but I thought I'd just seen Ruby's favourite client.

I left the saloon before I got to see her face.

FIVE

Any thought that Tug was doing me a favour by offering me a job was soon forgotten when I turned up at his yard and started work. I was hoping that Nancy might have improved his nature, but he seemed to be forever barking orders at everyone, especially me. Some of the men didn't help matters by teasing him about his reunion with Nancy and saying how tired he was looking. There was lots of talk about a second honeymoon and warm beds.

The men were decent enough, except Tug's buddies who I'd encountered yesterday. They seemed to be suspicious of me for some reason, perhaps because they weren't as dumb as Tug and knew that Nancy was a schemer.

By the time I'd finished my first day stacking the smaller logs I was aching all over, but the wound to my arm hadn't bothered me and I no longer felt weak. Some of the younger fellers invited me along to the saloon and I said I would catch up with them later. One of them had remembered a feller who could have been Kelsall being thrown out of the saloon for cheating at cards just a couple of nights ago.

My intention of not eating for a week was soon forgotten and I headed for Charlie's diner. The place was empty and Mick gave me a warm greeting after he stopped drinking what I assumed was black coffee from a large glass.

'You look all in, feller. I take it you found a job.'

When I told him I was working for Tug, he frowned.

'He's a big ape that one, but he's as soft as cow shit. I can give you a tip about him just in case you ever tangle with him. Make sure you hit him in his big fat belly. There's no point in going for his face because he's got a head of solid bone, and he's fond of using it, so beware of that.'

Mick explained that he had the scars to prove Tug's practice of head butting and rubbed his broad, bent nose.

'But I got the better of the bastard and they ended up taking him home on a cart. He's never been in here since. The cheeky sod only tried to sup my precious liquor, my liquid gold as I call it. Here, have a sip. It's my own special brew and beats that piss they serve in the saloons in this town.'

I took a small sip, followed by a gulp when Mick encouraged me have a proper drink.

'What do you think?' he asked, curious to know my reaction.

'It's good,' I answered and meant it. It had a smoothness about it and yet it was a strong taste.

By the time Mick waved me on my way I had consumed one of his meals, a single one this time and washed it down with four large glasses of his special beer. I had only ever been drunk once before, but this time it felt different. I think Motty must have sensed something different about me because he snorted more than usual when I rode him to the livery. He even gave several more snorts before I left him and headed for the saloon to meet up with my three new working buddies. There were smiles all round when I offered to buy them a drink.

'I think you've had a head start on us, partner,' said Clem, the youngest of my new-found buddies.

'Perhaps he's been drinking Tug's beer at home with Nancy while the big man is still at work,' said Donny, and winked at the others.

'Well he's not fit for pleasuring her now,' remarked Clem, and they all laughed.

By the time I finished my third drink, or maybe it was the fourth, things were getting a bit hazy and everything I said seemed to amuse the others.

SIX

I heard the distant banging and thought there must be a fire in the hotel and then I wondered who the naked woman was as she went to open the door. I saw the man with the marshal's badge at about the same time that I realized that I wasn't in my hotel room.

The marshal drew his pistol and asked me if I'd brought Nancy into town yesterday.

I nodded without speaking because I was looking at the woman sitting on the bed staring at my nakedness. I made an unsuccessful attempt to pull the sheet over me, but she was sitting on it.

'What's your name, mister?' the marshal asked.

I told him and he said that he was arresting me for murder. My mind was beginning to clear. I couldn't be certain that I hadn't murdered someone because I couldn't remember much after I'd met up with the boys. The only thing I could think of was that someone had killed Tug and I was getting the blame.

'I'm arresting you for the murder of Hank Ellison out at his cabin. So make yourself decent before we go downstairs unless you want the whole saloon to see what Ruby's gawping at.'

'He's got nothing to be ashamed of, Marshal,' Ruby said, and added, 'I was looking forward to him sobering up and now you've spoiled my fun.'

'Shut up, Ruby, and make yourself decent as well. Those droopy tits of yours are putting me off my supper. And when are you going to stop wearing that silly eye patch? Everyone knows that you've got two good eyes.'

'You didn't complain about my tits last week when you came here for a free one,' Ruby snapped. 'I seem to remember you saying that you dreamed about touching them.' She fidgeted with her eye patch, but didn't remove it.

Marshal Hollinger tried to cover his discomfort by ordering his deputy Ned Steele to pick up my pistol from the floor.

At least they smuggled me out the back to avoid me further embarrassment after Ruby had shouted that the next time would be on the house. Within a few minutes of leaving the saloon I was pushed into one of the two tiny cells in the marshal's office opposite the saloon. I don't know how long I'd been in the room with Ruby, but according to my late pa's watch it was just coming up to ten o'clock. I lay on the thin mattress, which appeared to be clean, and racked my brain to try and remember my time in the bar with Donny and his friends. I would probably never forget that Ruby had no teeth and was too old to have been my ma. I had faint recollection about there being a mention of her having a glass eye, but perhaps that had been part of a bad dream. I would discover later that Ruby would charge extra to any curious cowboy who wanted to see what was under the patch. I also learned that she was carrying a disease. So maybe the drink had saved me from a lot of itching, or something more serious. I even managed a smile when I thought that being infected by Ruby was the least of my problems, because it wouldn't matter none if I was going to end up dangling from the end of a rope.

My thoughts were interrupted when Deputy Steele pushed a small tin mug of lukewarm coffee under the bars of the cell. Marshal Hollinger was behind him and he wanted to know if I was ready to confess. He didn't seem to be interested when I told him that I didn't kill Hank and that he was alive when I rode away from his property yesterday.

'Why don't you ask Nancy?' I pleaded. 'She can back me up. She knows that Hank was alive when I left because she was there with him.'

'If that's your defence then you're going to hang

because I went to see Nancy after old Jeremiah Doolan brought Hank's shot-up body into town a few hours ago, and she told me a different story.'

According to the marshal, Nancy had told him that I ordered her to ride off while I was fighting with Hank. Nancy claimed that was the last she saw of Hank and when I caught up with her I told her not to worry because Hank wouldn't be bothering her ever again.

My mind was too muddled to make anything of this, except that Nancy must have murdered Hank and was now putting the blame on me. I asked what would happen to my horse and the marshal said it would be taken care of until the trial next week and he would have his deputy pick up my things from the hotel.

Despite my predicament I managed to sleep until daylight, but then my nightmare came flooding into my mind. I could picture Ruby perfectly now and I shook my head in some hopeless attempt to erase her from my memory. She had probably been beautiful once, but now she was an old hag. I had some vague memories of Donny joking about her after I had produced my voucher with the number eight and the name Ruby on it. That was the last thing I remembered until the marshal started banging on the door and arrested me.

It was mid afternoon when the marshal told me

that I had a visitor. I rose from my bed, hoping that it was Nancy and that she had come to explain and get me out of here. It was Mick and he had brought some food with him.

'What's all this about, young feller? I've just told the marshal that you aren't a killer. If you were, then you would hardly have come and stayed so close to where Hank lived.'

'The scheming little, bitch,' was all Mick said, after I had given him my version of events. He shook his head and added, 'The problem is, son, it'll be her word against yours and the lily-livered jury in this town would rather side with Tug's wife than a stranger like you.'

Before Mick left he told me he planned to go and see old Jeremiah who'd found Hank's body, just in case he might be able to help, but he couldn't see how. He also promised to bring some more grub tomorrow. I didn't want to seem ungrateful by telling him that I had no stomach for food right now.

Deputy Steele wasn't much older than me and helped me take my mind off things by playing cards. He asked me if I really had done it with One Eyed Ruby and when I asked, 'Would you?' he replied, 'I've never been that drunk.'

SEVEN

It was mid-morning and my second day in the cell when Mick arrived and started arguing with the marshal and they were still shouting when they left the office together. Deputy Steele said that they were going to see the bank manager, but he didn't know why.

When the marshal and Mick returned they had another man with them, who I would discover later was Jeremiah Doolan. Whatever the fuss was about earlier it seemed to have been resolved, because this time everything was calm when they all approached my cell.

'You are free to go, son,' said the marshal, and then advised me to leave town today. It seemed that Tug had been making threats against me because he believed that I had something going with Nancy.

I was stunned to hear that I was free to leave and

could hardly believe it, but I gathered my bits and pieces and made my way out of the cell.

Mick had a broad smile on his face and shook me by the hand. The marshal said that I had to thank Mick and old Jeremiah, who looked as though he had started drinking early.

'So did you help prove that Nancy killed Hank?' I asked.

'Nancy didn't kill him,' Mick answered, and then continued, 'Let's go to the diner and I'll rustle you up some grub before you leave. Jeremiah can come as well and then I can explain everything to you.'

The marshal shook my hand and said he was sorry. Deputy Steele smiled and said, 'You're a mean card player, Sam. Stay lucky.'

When I sat down in front of a Mick-special, he explained that when he went to see Jeremiah, the old-timer showed him a note that he'd found near Hank's body. Jeremiah meant to give it to the marshal, but he forgot. It was Hank's suicide note in which he said he couldn't face living without Nancy. There was an empty whiskey bottle beside him. He must have got drunk and then shot himself. When Mick showed the note to the marshal earlier he said that I could have written the note. So they went to the bank and compared the handwriting with the writing on some documents that Hank had lodged there. The marshal agreed that Hank had written the suicide note while depressed after a heavy bout of drinking.

I thanked Mick for all that he'd done. He might not be a great speller, but thanks to his reading skills I had escaped a hanging. Jeremiah seemed too busy tucking into his food to take much notice when I thanked him as well.

Mick said he had been doing some thinking and suggested that Kelsall might have joined up with the cattle drive that had left a few days ago. They would be stopping at the medium-sized town of Dyer's Gulch which was just over a day's hard ride from here. I collected Motty and we headed out of a town that I would never forget. It was the town where I had almost ended my days.

I rode until dark apart from one short stop to water Motty and camped near a sheltered spot amongst some pine trees. I made sure that I kept my pistol close by because I wasn't convinced about Mick's reasoning that Sharkey was many miles from here.

EIGHT

I was awakened by the morning sun that shone through a gap in the trees and was soon preparing to move on. Mick had given me some money to tide me over and said that he trusted me to repay him, and hoped it would be in person. I settled for a mug of coffee and a chunk of cheese and was soon on my way. I was confident that providing nothing unforeseen happened I should be clear of the mountain trail before it was too dark to ride, and with luck I would be in Dyer's Gulch before nightfall.

By noon I had passed through some of the most rugged land I had ever ridden and if my map was accurate, I wasn't too far from the mountain trail, so I opted to keep going. The note on the map indicated that the lower trail didn't involve much climbing, but I still intended to take it easy.

It had been some hours since my last stop when I sensed that old Motty was beginning to struggle. I was about to dismount when I saw a wooden sign that pointed to another trail that led to a higher level. It read: *Cheap Grub Served All Day*. A smaller sign underneath indicated that it was only a hundred yards away. I'd been a bit greedy tucking into Mick's food pack as I rode, and the thought of extra food so close by was too tempting, and it would give Motty the chance to rest. So, I pulled on the reins and guided Motty on to the higher trail hoping I would soon be tucking into some food.

I was at the point of thinking that it was a long hundred yards and that diner in the mountains might have been long gone, when I caught a whiff of cooking. Then I saw the burning fire through a gap in the rocks and I was a mite pleased.

'Come on in, young feller,' beckoned the man sitting by the fire. He had a resemblance to old Jeremiah. The same stoop, longish nose and a thatch of white hair, except this feller had a beard to match and his eyes were sunk into his skull.

The 'diner' consisted of a table and couple of chairs set in a large enclosure that stretched back towards the base of a small mountain. I spotted what must have been an entrance to a cave. The man raised a small bony hand and introduced himself as Indigo Sage. It was a strange name, but then again he must be a strange man to run a diner in a spot like this. I told him my name and asked if he did much business.

'Enough to keep me busy,' he replied. 'My nephew delivers me fresh meat once a week and it works out just about right for the number of men that use the mountain trail. By the way, I only dish up meat and there's only water to drink.'

I said that was fine seeing as I had a liking for a nice tender steak. I was surprised to see that two large steaks were already sizzling in a large skillet he was holding over the fire. Perhaps he had seen me coming or he had a big appetite for a little feller.

'These should be done in a couple of minutes. That's if you can afford them at fifty cents each,' he said, and then gave an odd chuckle. I said that one would be fine if he wanted the other one.

'I can cook the stuff, but I can never eat it. Those juicy beauties are both for you,' he said and told me to take a seat at the table that was covered with a check patterned tablecloth just like I'd seen in just about every diner I'd ever been in.

I was soon tucking into my unexpected treat. The first one was pretty good, but the second one was as tough as old boots, but at least my knife was razor sharp. I'd seen the old feller's few remaining teeth and so perhaps it was just as well that he didn't like meat. When he offered me some water from a dirty old mug I told him that I had a liking for coffee and would have some at my next stop. This caused him to give one of his strange chuckles. He didn't seem to want to talk much so I thought it was time for me to move on. I paid him an extra fifty cents and was preparing to climb up on Motty when he called out.

'Before you go, I'd be obliged if you could help me pull up some meat from where I store it in that old shaft over there. Its amazing how much colder it is below ground.'

I let Motty's reins drop, and replied, 'No problem,' and watched Indigo hobble in the direction of the thick wooden supports of the shaft that were sticking about three feet above the ground. Indigo asked me to undo the piece of rope that was tied to a peg in the ground and heave the meat out As my hand reached the end of the rope I cried out in surprise as I fell forward. Had Indigo not pushed me so hard I would have pitched head long down the shaft, but the force of the shove allowed me to reach out to the far side of the shaft and because of my lanky body I ended up straddled across it. Despite his gammy leg Indigo quickly scampered around the other side of the hole and started stamping on my fingers. I would have soon fallen into the shaft had I not grabbed his scrawny ankle and caused him to topple. I dug my fingernails into the earth as his bony body fell on to my back.

'Help me,' he screeched. I started to lose my grip again as he tried to crawl along my body to safety. I arched my back in an attempt to stop myself from sliding to my certain death. Indigo must have released his grip on me and tried to reach out for safety, causing him to slip from my back and plunge down the deep shaft, screaming as he fell. I lay stretched across the shaft, frozen in fear, realizing how close I had come to suffering the same fate as Indigo. As I slowly edged forward I braced myself for the moment when my legs would drop into the shaft, hoping I could hold on and then drag myself up. When it happened I cried out as I started sliding very slowly back towards the shaft. I clung on to a clump of a wild plant, and thought I was safe until it started to uproot, but I managed to heave my way out and then lay on my back, exhausted.

When my gasping stopped I heard the faint groan from the shaft, indicating that Indigo must have survived. I scrambled to my feet and peered down the dark shaft. There was no reply when I called out to him, but as my eyes became accustomed to the darkness I saw a body that appeared to be dangling from the rope. It looked as though Indigo had somehow landed on to the meat that he'd asked me to haul out.

I took my own rope from the cantle of Motty's saddle and tied it to the end of the one that was secured to the peg that was driven well into the ground. Indigo was only skin and bone but he would be a dead weight so I knew it wouldn't be easy, especially as I would be hauling up the stored meat as well. I would try pulling him up myself first. I scraped a small channel in the earth and dug my heels into it. I paused between pulls on the rope, but I was sweating heavily by the time that the head appeared. I almost let the rope slip from my hands when I saw that it wasn't Indigo but the body of a young man. I hauled him out on to the ground beside the shaft. The back of his head was caved in, his hair matted with dried blood and one of his legs had been hacked off.

The man hadn't been dead very long and I began retching and then spewed against the rocks when I realized that my juicy steaks had probably been part of the man's missing leg. I wiped away the vomit from my mouth once I had stopped trying to empty my stomach My instinct was to ride away and try to forget what I'd experienced, but I couldn't leave without burying the body. The depraved Indigo could rot where he was. Not that I could have recovered his body from the shaft on my own because he was too far down to try and grab at with a makeshift hook.

I managed to find a shovel, but really needed a

pickaxe because of the hardness of the ground. I finally settled for a reasonable depth and then piled some small rocks on top of the grave to prevent any vultures getting at the body. I decided to take a look in the cave just in case Indigo might have imprisoned some other victims in his mountain hideaway.

When I got within ten feet of the cave entrance the stench hit me and I covered my mouth with my neckerchief As I stepped inside I saw a bony horse which was barely alive. I drew my pistol and held it against its head and ended the wretched animal's life. The horse fell to the ground and now I could see a pile of human skeletons, some clothed. I stepped over the horse for a closer view. Most of them had been men, judging by their clothes, but one had been a woman with long hair who was next to a young girl with a pink ribbon in her hair. I nearly tripped over the dead horse as I hurried from the cave and began vomiting again, but this time only bile came up and my stomach ached with each retch.

NINE

I was eager to get to Dyer's Gulch which Indigo had told me was less than three miles away because I needed to report what had happened to the marshal and then I would look for Kelsall. Had I known that the town was so close I might have ridden on and avoided the horror of what I'd experienced! It was likely that the neglected horse that I'd finished off had been Indigo's, but what had happened to the horses of the poor souls? The ones who had been pushed down the shaft or bludgeoned from behind by the evil little man with the strange cackle! There was a possibility that Indigo had an accomplice who disposed of the horses and belongings of the victims.

I started to head Motty down a trail that led out the other side to which I had entered the hideaway, but decided to go back down the same way I came in and remove the sign. I wouldn't want an unsuspecting traveller deciding to seek some food like I did and end up seeing the gruesome sights. I was soon regretting my decision when Motty snorted and nearly unseated me as he reared up in distress. My first thought was that he'd been bitten by a snake.

When I dismounted I could see that he was holding his right fore hoof off the ground and there was blood dripping from it. I took my bowie knife from the saddle-bag and lay on the ground near the troublesome leg, hoping that I could remove the sharp stone that must have penetrated the skin between the rims of the shoe. The blood was dripping faster and some of it dropped on to my face as I positioned myself to get a closer look The problem wasn't a stone, but a shard of bone. I wondered if it had been part of some unfortunate victim of Indigo that had been dragged there by an animal and buried. I had no way of telling how deep the bone had penetrated, but there might just be enough left protruding for me to be able to grip it and pull it out with my fingers. My first attempt had Motty reacting in a way that meant I was causing him more harm than good and I was thinking that my fingers were not suited for such a tricky operation. At the rate the blood was coming out of the wound Motty might be dead by the time I came back with some help from the town. It seemed that the kindest thing would be to finish him off like I'd done the horse in the cave. I was about to have one final attempt at removing the bone when I noticed a small hook shape on one side of it. I placed the point of my knife in the hook and told Motty to hang on and then steadied myself ready to try and pull it out, knowing that I could only try this once. There was a slurping noise as the bone eased out slowly, causing yet more blood to spill on to my hand. Luckily the bone was fully removed before Motty reared up, and I managed to roll to one side avoiding him landing on me.

'Jesus,' I said, as I saw that the bone was nearly two inches long and most of it had been in Motty's hoof. It was no more than half an inch at its widest and tapered to a point, but judging by the amount of fresh blood I might have made matters worse and caused Motty extra pain for nothing. I scrambled to my feet and fumbled in my saddle-bag for my spare shirt and tore it into strips to use to try and stem the flow of blood. Motty made my task easier by standing still, no doubt sensing that I was trying to help him. By the time I'd finished applying my makeshift bandages it looked as though his hoof was in a large boot which he gingerly placed on the ground. This stroke of bad luck left me with a problem. I couldn't ride or even walk Motty to the town and the surrounding terrain wasn't suitable for resting him up. I had no choice, but to take Motty back the short distance to the hideaway and rest him there for the night.

I led him as gently as I could up the trail and was soon at the scene of my earlier dice with death where Indigo tried to push me down the shaft. The fire was still burning and I tossed some small logs on to it. For some reason I was shivering even though the sun was shining and it was still only early autumn. I had no experience of life in the mountains. I knew it would be cold, but not this cold; perhaps I was sickening for something. I gathered some dry clothes from the cave, trying to avoid looking at the human remains, spread them on the ground and then persuaded Motty to lie on them.

When Motty had settled down I ventured through a passage in the rocks situated to the right of the shaft and discovered a series of other caves. The first one must have been where Indigo had lived judging by the simple furniture in there. The next one was full of saddles, pistols, blankets, pots and pans and an assortment of other items that had probably belonged to Indigo's victims.

I entered the last cave with some dread when I saw a trail of what looked like dried blood outside. The makeshift table made from stacked rocks was covered with a bloodstained blanket and once again I was regretting my curiosity when I saw the man's boot containing the butchered remnants of the lower part of a leg. Before I retreated from the cave I'd noticed a number of knives, axes and a bloodstained saw. I think it was a fair bet that the foot belonged to the man that I'd buried a few hours earlier and whose flesh I had chewed with such relish.

I made my way back to the passage that linked to the main area and stopped at the two wooden crosses that had caught my attention earlier. The details etched in the blocks of wood revealed that Indigo's wife, and 10-year-old daughter were buried here. A third piece of wood contained the message: *They were left to die by merciless men. They will be avenged* and it looked to have been placed there recently.

The chilling message had me being curious again and I decided to have a closer look in Indigo's cave. It seemed hard to believe that an evil son of a bitch like him could have been a family man. I discovered more knives, but these had been used for wood carving judging by the selection of small wooden horses and some other animals that I didn't recognize. I didn't feel any guilt snooping through Indigo's belongings because I didn't aim to steal anything. I opened the small wooden chest that had been concealed by a pile of wood and discovered that it contained papers and so I carried it back to the fire. I checked Motty's hoof and then sat by the warmth and started reading through the papers. By the time I closed the chest it was getting dark and I'd discovered that Indigo Sage, his wife Ruth and daughter Bethany had been planning a new life in this territory nearly twenty years ago. It appeared that his wife and daughter must have died close by. Judging by some of the items in his living-quarters he was a skilled wood carver, but the papers revealed that he had once worked as a butcher.

TEN

The sun had been up for a while when I threw the blankets to one side and stretched the stiffness from by body. I'd heard Motty make the odd noise during the night, but I'd been surprised when I'd glanced over towards him earlier and seen that he was up and standing on all four legs. I'd heard other noises during the night coming from the direction of the shaft or should I say the body cave! I'd had a dream in which Indigo Sage clawed his way out of the shaft and attacked me with an axe while I slept. I suspected the noises had been caused by some animals scavenging for food, mainly human remains. I'd kept my boots on, but at one point I was convinced that something was chewing my big toe.

An inspection of Motty's injury and a quick test walking him around made me decide that I would walk him into Dyer's Gulch, but first I needed to start the fire, make some coffee and finish the remains of the food that Mick had given me. There was plenty of water trickling down the mountain and Indigo had built a contraption of pipes to direct the water into two troughs. Motty had already dipped his head into one of them and his slurping seemed to echo around the place.

I forgot to mention that tucked away at the bottom of the chest containing the papers was a tidy stack of dollar bills, amounting to $7,500, to be exact. I intended to hand the money over to the marshal in Dyer's Gulch, but I would make sure there was a witness when I did.

I'd already walked down the trail and removed the notice pointing to cheap grub that had enticed me here yesterday. The marshal might decide not to do anything about my findings and without the notice the place might remain undiscovered for a very long time.

I took a last look around then led Motty down what I hoped would be the easier trail and was relieved to discover it was a wise choice. Once clear of the mountains the view opened up and I could see the town of Dyer's Gulch below. It was only supposed to be about three miles away, but it looked much further and I hoped Motty would make it.

When we reached the level ground I stopped at

regular intervals to check on Motty and wasn't surprised to see that the wound had started bleeding again, but it had barely seeped through cloth that I'd bound tightly around it and so I continued.

We were within half a mile of town when our trail was joined by another one and we encountered a steady stream of riders heading in the same direction as we were. The riders seemed in high spirits, but some shouted some cruel remarks about Motty and one even offered to shoot him.

We were about to enter Dyer's Gulch's main street when a wagon passed by heading out of town. The anxious-looking man shouted down to me, 'I wouldn't go into that town, mister. Not unless your life depends on it.' The rest of what he said was drowned by the thunder of hoofs as a large group of cowboys passed by. Some began firing shots into the air, but it didn't seem to spook Motty.

My first call was John's Livery which was just at the beginning of Main Street, but I was in for a disappointment when I saw the 'Closed' sign on the large wooden doors.

'Damn,' I cursed out loud, but still led Motty up to the doors. Then I started unwrapping the remnants of my shirt from around the wound. There was a fair amount of dried blood on the cloth, but there was no sign of an infection.

'How did that happen, mister?' said the guy who'd crossed from over the street. I didn't want to get into the details so I told him that it must have been a sliver of rock.

'That's a nasty cut,' he observed after studying it.

I asked if there was anyone in town who might be able to look at it, perhaps the doc if they had one. I was surprised by his answer.

'I'm the nearest thing to what you're looking for. Bring him around the back and I'll patch him up.

I thanked him and asked him if he was John.

'No, I'm Matt. John was my pa. He was gunned down by some drunken cowboys about this time last year when the cattle drive came nearby. That's why I've closed up, because they'll be in town for the next couple of days.'

The mention of the cattle drive had me thinking of Kelsall and I felt a strange feeling of excitement and a bit of fear I guess. I wondered if Matt's hatred of cattlemen was greater than mine for Kelsall.

Matt looked to be about thirty something, had a full beard and was the first livery man I'd seen packing two pistols. He quickly mixed some foul smelling concoction and then gently applied it to the wound before covering it with a soft white pad. He finished the job off by tightly wrapping a long strip of sacking material around the hoof and up about six inches of the lower leg.

'It looks a lot neater than my shirt bandage did. Where did you learn how to do that?' I regretted asking the question when he told me that his pa had taught him all he knew about treating horse injuries as well as blacksmithing.

Matt said that Motty could stay until he'd recovered at a charge of a dollar a day and that included treatment and food. He thought it would be between three and five days before he would be well enough to ride. I handed over the five dollars wondering where I was going to sleep tonight and asked him if I could bed down in the livery. He said he was sorry, but he never allowed it since a drunken cowboy had nearly burnt the place down when he'd dropped his cigar in the hay.

Before I left the livery I asked him if he knew Indigo and where could I find the marshal.

'Just about everyone knows Indigo or Mountain Man as he's called. He's a strange one and that's a fact. I don't know what he does up there in the mountains, but he comes into town every once in awhile even though he doesn't buy much, or say much for that matter. You'll find Marshal Johnson's office opposite the Malted Whiskey Saloon, but he might be in one of the other saloons keeping an eye out for troublemakers.'

'Is the marshal trustworthy?' I asked.

'That's an odd question to ask, stranger, but let's

say they don't come any better than Seth Johnson. I'd trust him with my best horse if that helps you any.'

'It does,' I answered, and then decided to confide in the man who had been a big help to me. I told him that Indigo was dead and that I had sort of killed him, but it was an accident. I ended up telling him the whole gruesome details and about the stash of money that I intended to hand over to the marshal.

'I've never heard such a gruesome tale. You must have been through hell up there last night. A lot of men would have bought another horse and got the hell out of here. I guess you must have been brought up by some real decent folks. If you want me to, I'll go along with you to see the marshal and sort of introduce you.'

'It would make things easier for me if it's not too much trouble.'

'No problem,' he replied. He asked me my name and we were soon on our way to the marshal's office, with me carrying the saddle-bag containing Indigo's ill-gotten gains. I took the opportunity to ask him about Kelsall, but he couldn't help, except to say that there would be a lot of gambling going on in town over the next few days.

Marshal Seth Johnson looked worried when we entered his office and he asked Matt if he'd come to report some trouble with the cowboys. He relaxed when Matt said there was no trouble, but that I needed to talk to him.

Seth Johnson was a powerfully built man of about 50, I would guess. He had steely grey hair, pale-blue eyes and a broad nose that had escaped being broken, but his face was badly scarred. One scar was dark blue and ran the full length of his left cheek. Matt introduced me and when I repeated my story about Indigo it drew a sharp reaction from the marshal.

'Jesus, you're not kidding me, are you, boy?'

'I wish I was, Marshal,' I replied, and noticed that the young deputy who had been listening had gone pale. The marshal shook his head and then said that my story fitted in with some of the accounts that men passing through had told about the amazing diner in the mountains. It looked as though those men had had a lucky escape and the marshal said that it was probably because they weren't travelling alone. He also remarked that there had been some enquiries about missing people, but that happened all over the territory.

The young deputy, Joel Lines, had recovered from my gruesome description and he used the marshal's favourite phrase of 'Jesus' when the marshal took the wad of notes and spread them on the desk and said, 'Either Indigo butchered some rich folks who ventured into his trap or a hell of lot of not so rich ones.'

Marshal Johnson played with the bundle of notes like it was a deck of cards and he seemed to be pondering what to do. When he ordered young Joel to go and fetch the mayor and Milton Small who ran the bank I guessed he'd decided.

As soon as the deputy had left the office the marshal began counting the money and placed some of it in a smaller pile. I have to confess that my first thought was that he was going to split some of the money between us. So much for Matt's praise that the marshal was trustworthy, I thought.

'The way I see this,' the marshal began, 'there's no way that this money can be returned to its rightful owners. So young, feller, I want you to take that five hundred dollar pile for your honesty. Think of it as a reward. I'll tell the mayor about it later. It will be up to him and the town council what they do with the rest of it.'

I tried to refuse, but the marshal insisted that I took it and said that he had a little job for me to do, but he'd explain after the mayor had left.

The meeting with the mayor didn't last long and the bank manager seemed pleased with the $7,000 he was asked to place in the bank. The marshal had told the mayor that once the cowboys had left town he would take some men up to Indigo's place and bury the bodies from the cave. Indigo and any poor souls at the bottom of the shaft would remain there forever because the marshal intended to dynamite the shaft and turn it into a tomb. The bad news was that the marshal wanted me to show them where the place was. When I protested, the marshal reminded me that I'd thrown away the sign pointing the way to Indigo's and without my help they would struggle to find it. It seemed a poor excuse for taking me along but I didn't argue with him.

Matt said he planned carrying on guarding the livery and he would look in on Motty. He turned down my offer of help to guard the place and I intended to take his advice and enjoy myself. Thanks to the $500 I was able to book into Ryman's Hotel, which was the best in town and then I went and had a bath, shave, and got myself kitted out with some new clothes.

ELEVEN

It was just after eight o'clock when I'd finished a modest dinner at Larry's Diner before I set out to check the saloons. Larry had seemed puzzled when I declined his specialty steak and settled for eggs and beans. I'd done a bit of reflecting while I'd been at the diner and decided that if Kelsall didn't turn up here then I would head home. I needed to tell Grandpa about Jack and then I would go after Kelsall again. In the meantime I didn't see any harm in trying to enjoy myself some. I didn't want to look back and think that I'd wasted my opportunity while I was away from home. I was known by just about everyone in the town where I was born and that sort of limited my fun, but for the moment I could do what I wanted. So tonight I would choose myself a saloon girl. If I gave the impression that I'd already sampled one, then I lied, apart from Ruby, but you remember what happened there – nothing. I would go easy on the drink, remembering what I'd heard about drinking and pleasuring a woman not mixing. But I also wanted to have another go at gambling, but this time I would quit before I lost too much.

Bootles Saloon had more bodies than I'd ever seen in one place, most of the men seemed to have drunk too much already and I'd spotted a couple of the saloon girls even refuse business from some of them. I got myself a beer after a struggle at the bar and made sure I could get a good view of the girl who I'd heard someone call Isobel. She was probably about my age, and even more stunning than some of the girls I'd seen in Bothey Waters. I would normally have felt awkward when she smiled at me, but I didn't. I think it was probably the relief of my recent experiences and the thought of not wanting to regret missed chances.

There were two card games in progress, one had a vacant seat and I was invited to join when I approached the table. It would give me a good opportunity to keep a lookout for Kelsall. I noticed on my walk over from the diner that there was a steady stream of trail boys arriving in town.

I was bit taken aback to see that one of the players in the card game was Milton Small, the bank manager I'd met earlier, and the three others looked equally businesslike. Perhaps it was my new clothes that impressed them, or maybe they decided that I looked like a young loser. Milton Small explained the rules and the stake limits and they all smiled when I placed my stake money on the table, perhaps in anticipation of winning it from me. I might have forgotten to mention that on the night that I lost my horse at a card game I was as drunk as a skunk.

By the time I'd lost my third game in a row and was fifty dollars down I was thinking that I might try my luck with Isobel, but she was involved in a conversation with some evil-looking dude so I stayed in the game and tried to stop myself from looking in her direction. Five games later I had recovered my fifty dollars and was now almost $100 up. One of the players had dropped out before the next game which was a humdinger between me and the bank manager. When the pot reached $200 we had an audience around our table and one of the onlookers was Isobel. I was having trouble taking my eyes off her as she stood opposite me, leaning forward, to make sure that I could see her heavy breasts that looked as though they were about to pop out of her dress.

'Are you losing interest in this game, sir?' Milton Small asked me. He was sure getting jumpy and his chubby face was sweating some.

I apologized and raised him $100. He fidgeted with his collar, fumbled with his stake money and then asked to see my cards. I didn't like him much and so I took my time in displaying my cards, knowing that they were unbeatable.

He muttered something about beginner's luck, collected his remaining money off the table and left. The crowd melted away, now that the game was over, except Isobel who sat down at the table.

'Are you?' she asked.

I smiled back at her and replied, 'Am I what?'

She paused, and moved her tongue slowly over her top lip before answering, 'A beginner.'

I gathered up my pile of money and showed it to her. 'What do you think?'

'My question was about making love, not playing cards,' she said.

I was on the point of losing my new-found confidence when she suggested that if I parted with some of my winnings we could go to her room upstairs and she would find out the answer.

I asked if I could buy her a drink first which prompted her to smile as she came around to me and whispered in my ear, 'If it is going to be your first time then we don't want too much drink to spoil it, do we?' I stood up without answering and she put an arm around my waist and led me away from the table in the direction of the stairs. I looked over my shoulder and my eyes scanned the bar for Kelsall to ease my guilt that I hadn't done more to see if he was in town before I started thinking of enjoying myself.

As soon as she closed the door she kissed me and pressed her body tightly against my crotch. She might be doing this for money, but she seemed to be enjoying it. She broke away from me and started to unbutton my shirt, pausing as she tapped my pistol and said that I wouldn't be needing it. I mumbled an awkward apology, unbuckled my belt and placed it on the chair beside the bed which she had slowly edged us towards. She invited me to unfasten her dress and I'm sure my fumbling removed any doubt she might have had about me being a beginner. I made things worse by asking her how much she wanted. At the moment I would have probably given her every last cent I had, which was a tidy sum.

Isobel had peeled back the top of her dress to reveal her naked breasts and then lay back on the pillow. Her nipples were much larger than I'd imagined, showing as dark brown circles in the middle of her milky white skin, and they were pointed, or is the word, erect! I leaned forward to kiss her and she placed a finger on my lips and quietly answered my question about paying her, 'Shush, just leave me something in the morning, but only if you enjoy yourself,' and then she started undoing my pants.

I gasped with excitement before turning towards the door and then felt the full force of the pistol handle that struck me across the side of the face.

My head hurt like hell, but the pillow was soft and I could smell the perfume, and then I remembered Isobel. I reached out to feel if she was beside me.

I heard a voice, but it wasn't Isobel's. I forced my eyes open and saw Deputy Joel Lines.

'Marshal, he's awake,' he called out.

'He hasn't been asleep, you big dope,' said Marshal Johnson, as he came closer to the bed. Then he asked me how my cheek was. I hadn't felt it until he asked, but now it was throbbing and I remembered seeing the pistol coming towards me.

'Is Isobel all right?' I asked, ignoring the marshal's question, concerned for her wellbeing.

'She's doesn't deserve any sympathy, young feller,' he replied, and then added, 'She's being well looked after until she leaves town on the stage-coach tomorrow.'

I sat up and asked him what he was doing in Isobel's room and what was going on.

He explained that the no-good dude who pistol whipped me, also stole all my money. I groaned at the loss, but I was still concerned about Isobel and asked him again if she was all right.

'You really are a greenhorn, son. Isobel was in cahoots with Drew Simpson, the feller who stole your money, who is also her husband. They are both locked up in the cells. Simpson will be going to prison and I've already told you she'll be leaving tomorrow. She can count herself lucky that she's not going to prison as well. The bitch won't be allowed back in this town for as long as I'm marshal.'

The marshal must have decided that he'd made me suffer long enough already and said, 'Don't worry, your money's locked up in my safe, all bar ten dollars. Now I suggest that you stay here for the night. Oh and by the way, the boys from the main cattle outfit have already left town. So things will be quieter from now on, which means that we can head out to Indigo's place tomorrow. Joel will pick you up at ten o'clock and fix you up with a horse. See you tomorrow.'

The lawmen made their way out of the room but not before Joel had grinned at me as he closed the door. I was left to ponder a night that had started so well and nearly ended in disaster. I didn't dwell on it for too long because I felt so sleepy. The bed was comfy enough, but I felt so hot. I struggled out of the bed and stripped off the rest of my clothes as well as my boots and then snuggled down again. I had no idea what time it was except judging by the noise, the saloon was still in full swing. I heard some argument and a woman screaming and then I fell asleep.

'It's all right. You've been dreaming, honey,' said

the sweet voice in my ear.

I opened my eyes. It was still dark and the town was asleep, no late night cowboys shouting, no dogs barking.

'Isobel, I thought you were. . . .' I turned over and felt the nakedness of a woman's body press against me.

I felt the moistness of soft lips and the probing of her tongue as it gently sought mine. I shuddered with excitement as her hand held me where I'd never be touched before, except maybe by Ruby when I knew nothing about it. I wanted to see her clearly, but the darkness meant I could see only an outline of her body. She had guided me on to my back and then sat astride me, sighing as we were joined. There was no awkwardness, no fumbling, just the helping hand of nature I suppose. There was enough light entering the room for me to see her dim shadow as she rode me, slowly at first and then quicker in time to her panting and then in a final gasp from both of us, it was over.

'I'm not a beginner anymore,' I told her, my voice sounding drowsy.

She must have sensed my tiredness and said that I should sleep now. I wondered if she found pleasure with all men and then I drifted to sleep, just as I was wondering why my cheek was hurting.

TWELVE

It might have been the sunlight shining through the window, the voices or the rumbling of a wagon passing by that woke me up. More likely it was the sound of her moving sround the room. She turned to face me just as I was about to call her name. She was beautiful, but she wasn't Isobel. My head was clear now. It couldn't have been Isobel who I had made love to during the night because she was in a cell across the street and my cheekbone was still throbbing.

She turned away from the mirror and faced me, smiled, walked over to the bed and kissed me lightly on the lips.

'I've got to go, lover,' she said, and walked towards the door.

'Did we, you know, make love?' I asked, and then explained that the blow to my face must have scrambled my brain, because I didn't know what was real and what was in my dreams.

She smiled and said, 'It was real all right, honey. My name's Maisey and Marshal Johnson paid me to keep you company last night.'

'Can I see you again? Can I buy you a present?' I asked, as she placed her hand on the door handle. I was disappointed when she replied that she didn't accept presents and it probably wasn't a good idea to see each other again. Then she was gone and I was left thinking about her warm, soft body. She wasn't unlike Isobel except that she was maybe five or so years older and her face was a bit harder.

I'd given myself a wash and dressed when there was a tap on the door. I was disappointed when Joel walked in and told me that the marshal and his party were heading out to Indigo's in half an hour. When he asked me which girl the marshal had arranged for me I told him to mind his own business.

'Unless it was Maisey, I'd make sure that you have a bath before we ride out.'

I didn't reply to his advice and he left, leaving me to take a final look at the bed before I headed back to my hotel to change into some working clothes. I had to step over a few sleeping cowboys as I made my way along the walkway from the saloon to the hotel. Some were lying in their own vomit, but one of them was cradling a post as though it was a woman. The sight of the cowboys had me feeling mighty guilty that I hadn't done more to find Kelsall last night as I realized that he might have been here and moved on.

I was outside the marshal's office within a few minutes, inspecting the grey mare that Joel had organized for me before I joined the party of six men counting the marshal and me. Joel had been told to hold the fort, but I thought the marshal might be protecting him from the scenes I'd described to them.

I rode alongside the marshal as we headed out of town and he frowned when I asked when the stagecoach would be leaving with Isobel on board, even though I already knew. He said that it was due out at midday and good riddance to her. He went on to explain that she hadn't been one of the regular girls and had only turned up the day before, just in time for the arrival of the cattle trail boys. He figured that she would have been leaving anyway if she and her husband had fleeced me or someone else. He said that I was lucky that one of the cowboys had fallen victim to her trick in Bothey Waters and warned him. When the marshal had burst into the room he'd been surprised to find me there and Simpson holding my money.

Two of the party had brought along wagons and they had to leave them when we reached the final trail to Indigo's and they followed on foot. One of them was even older than Grandpa and I couldn't see how he would be much use with any heavy work. I found out later that his name was Jim and he was some kind of expert with dynamite. I'd noticed that he hadn't been without a smouldering cigar in his mouth since we'd left town.

Marshal Johnson ordered one of the younger men to light a fire and told the party to stay put while I showed him around. As we reached the horror cave I pulled my neckerchief over my mouth and nose and suggested the marshal did the same thing. He didn't take my advice and was soon cursing and blaspheming, including his favourite word, Jesus.

The horse that I'd shot had provided a meal for something that had devoured chunks of its flesh, as well as both eyes, and a mass of flies were buzzing all over its remains. I'd never seen the little white wriggly things that looked like worms, but discovered later were maggots. The sight of the mother and daughter made even the hardened marshal decide that he'd seen enough for now and he left the cave.

By the time I had shown the marshal the other caves and the graves, the men had brewed some coffee, but I could have done with something stronger. Jim was the only one not near the fire and he was busy tying a stick of dynamite to each of the ropes that he'd strewn out near the shaft. The marshal shouted over to ask Jim if he would have any problems.

Jim took a long drag on his cigar before replying, 'Dynamitin' is never easy. I always say that dynamite sticks are just like a woman, unpredictable. I figure four sticks should be enough. We don't want to bring the mountain down on us, but it sure is going spook the horses.'

The marshal asked me to take two men to the cave and fetch the remains of the horse and dump it down the shaft. He agreed when I suggested that it might be a good idea if I covered the mother and daughter with some blankets first. So I went in search of the blankets and carried out my suggestion, wishing I'd kept my mouth shut.

When we staggered back with the horse there was bit of a commotion amongst the men who were standing near the shaft.

'I definitely heard something down there,' said Deputy Ty Kylie the youngest of the group. It prompted the marshal to ask me if there's any chance that Indigo could still be alive down there. I had to say that it was possible, but if he was, then he must be in one hell of state because of the depth of the shaft. One of the men asked what did it matter, he'd be dead soon when the horse landed on him or the shaft caved in after Jim had done his work. The marshal looked thoughtful and sent Ty to fetch a couple of oil lamps from one of the wagons.

While we waited for Ty to return, the marshal asked me to show Ben and Henry where the graves were and told them to dig two more and bury the mother and daughter I'd discovered in the cave.

Ty was puffing heavily when he returned with the lamps and the marshal began tying a rope around one lamp and ordered me to do the same with the other one. When the lamps were glowing we carried them towards the shaft, with the ropes trailing behind.

'OK, young feller. Start lowering your lamp on the left-hand side and I'll lower mine on the other side.'

I figured that the ropes were about twenty feet long and the lamps were just about fully lowered when I saw that Indigo only had one eye and it was staring up at me. It was only the remains of his distinctive waistcoat that made it possible to recognize him. The beady eyes of the rats that were feasting on him looked towards us, perhaps trying to decide whether we were a threat to them. They carried on eating and one of them began nibbling at Indigo's remaining eye. Whatever Ty had heard it wasn't Indigo, unless those critters down there hadn't eaten in a long time because most of his flesh on his face had already gone. The marshal and me had gasped, 'Jesus' at the same time and there were more to follow when the light of the lamps revealed that Indigo was on top of a mountain of human bones. I counted five skulls, one of which had some hair on it, before I started hoisting the lamp up without waiting for instructions from the marshal.

'What's down there, Marshal? Is Indigo alive?' Ty enquired.

'Indigo's dead, son, and you don't want to know what's down there,' answered the marshal and then ordered Jim to prepare to dynamite the shaft once the remains of the horse had been thrown in.

The marshal ordered everyone except Jim to leave and walk at least halfway down the trail. Jim had tied the ends of the ropes to four stakes in the ground. He'd explained earlier that the sticks would have to explode at the same time which meant that the first one that he lit was going to burn longer than the last one. Ty had looked a bit puzzled by the explanation and the marshal said he hoped that Jim wouldn't blow himself to kingdom come, wherever that was.

I asked the marshal if I could stay behind and watch Jim carry out the operation.

'I tell you, boy, you're dumber than you look,' he said, laughed and asked Jim if it was OK.

Jim said that he didn't mind, as long as I ran like billy-oh when he lit the fourth stick. He didn't say how he was going to manage to get clear because

I'd seen that he had a bad limp, and one of the men said he'd been in a mining accident!

After the others had gone, Jim told me to stand by the entrance that led to the other caves, and to run and take cover in the first cave once he'd lit the fourth stick. Jim turned and checked that I was in position before he blew on the end of his cigar while holding it against the first stick, which quickly fizzled like a firework I'd seen when I went on a trip back East as a boy. The second stick was soon fizzing away, but Jim was having trouble with the third one. I was thinking that he'd run out of puff as I watched him trying to get the stick to light. He threw his cigar away and used one of the fizzing sticks to light number three and four in succession and then hurled them into the shaft. I was too busy watching the ropes unfurl and Jim was running towards me before I turned and ran through the passageway. I don't know how he managed it, but Jim was right behind me as we entered the cave together. He sat down well inside the cave and suggested that I did the same.

'On the count of three,' he said, and then continued, 'one, two. . . .'

I am not sure if he got to say the final count because I only heard the massive bang and saw the table shake causing some of the contents on top of it to crash to the ground.

A broad smile spread across Jim's face, and he

reached into his pocket for a cigar.

'That was a scary moment back there when the third stick wouldn't light,' I said.

'These damn cheap cigars are to blame,' he growled, and then struggled to his feet ready to go and check his handiwork.

A cloud of dust and smoke was still rising from the shaft and so Jim suggested that we start a fresh brew of coffee and wait for the others to return. I could already hear the marshal shouting, asking if everything was all right. Jim put a finger across his mouth to signal me not to reply and then took my hat off my head and threw it near the shaft along with his. He winked and gestured for me to follow him.

We were safely hidden behind a large rock when he whispered for me to take off my boots and throw them near the hats.

The groans from Jim grew louder, but stopped long enough for us to hear Ty say, 'Shit, Marshal, one of them must have been blown out of his boots. These must belong to the young feller judging by the size.'

'I think we might have to bury their bits, if we can find them,' said the marshal who had obviously rumbled our little joke.

'Ty, go and look behind those rocks and see what you can find,' the marshal ordered.

Jim lay on his back, groaning, so I copied him

and joined in with my own bit of play-acting.

'They must be alive,' said Ty, and soon he and the marshal were staring down at us.

'Well, Jim's alive because he's still smoking those stinking cigars,' said the marshal and gave me a playful kick in the side.

'You two clowns should join the circus,' said the marshal and then added, 'I was really worried for a while until I saw the boots and hat. I think dopey Ty thought we would be scraping your bits off the mountain and taking them back to town wrapped in a blanket.'

We all laughed and went to check the shaft and discovered that the grisly contents were now entombed, just like Jim had planned. We drank our coffee and prepared to leave, but Jim had one more job to do as we left and that was to erect a few of his old notices near the entrance; one displayed: *Danger – Keep Out,* and the other *Dynamitin in Progress.*

We rode back to town in silence, perhaps all lost in our own thoughts. The marshal had told us that he would be making more trips to pick up the remaining items from the caves and said that the men would be well paid if they agreed to help him. I was relieved when he thanked me and said that my services wouldn't be needed.

When we reached John's livery the marshal told me to drop off my horse and said that if I came by his office later he would give me my money that he'd held for safekeeping since last night.

I was glad that Matt didn't ask me about the trip to the mountains and I was pleased when he said that Motty was well enough to ride now, which was sooner than expected. I told Matt some more about Kelsall and Cousin Jack and he promised to keep a look out, but reckoned that nearly all of the trail cowboys had already left town. Marshal Johnson had clamped down on them and barred the worst troublemakers from entering the saloons.

I told him that I would be heading home tomorrow to tell Grandpa about Jack, but I might come this way again when I restarted my search for Kelsall.

'Your grandpa will be glad to see that you are safe and might want you to forget about this Kelsall and leave him to the law.'

'It won't matter what Grandpa thinks, because I know I'll never settle if I didn't try again to capture or kill Sharkey Kelsall.'

'So I'd better have that drink with you tonight if the offer's still open,' said Matt, remembering my earlier suggestion.

I told Matt that I had something to attend to in town, but I would still like to buy him that drink tonight. I would make sure that I had searched the town high and low for Kelsall and then I would try and persuade Maisey to let me see her again. Perhaps if she knew that I was just passing through she might change her mind.

I followed the same routine as last night, except for the visit to the local store. So once I'd changed into my fancy new clothes I was soon tucking in at Larry's diner. When I placed the same order he looked disappointed and said, 'You're the feller that doesn't like meat. I've never known anyone not to like meat.' I told him that I had my reasons, but he wouldn't want to know what they were.

I nearly choked on my eggs and beans when he said later that I would change my mind if I ever sampled the meat supplied by an old-timer who lived in the mountains. I left the diner and headed for the saloon, thinking that when the word got out about Indigo, Larry would be shutting up shop and leaving town.

There wasn't a single horse tied to the hitch rail so I wasn't surprised to find that saloon was quiet compared to last night, now that the cattle-drive cowboys had moved on. I signalled a 'no' with my hand when Milton Small the bank manager beckoned me to join the card game. I would be a bit nervous about my money if I used his bank. I couldn't see any of the girls and hoped that was because it was still early. An hour later I was beginning to wonder if Matt was going to show, but I was more interested in whether Maisey would. I'd never considered that she might have a night off. Perhaps the girls had all done so much business with the cattle drive boys that they were all having a night off.

The curly-haired barman was a bit pushy in offering to refill my beer glass, but he was cheerful enough. When he passed me what must have been my sixth or seventh glass I asked what time the girls would be in. He looked up at the clock and announced that it would about another hour before things livened up and the girls would be in then.

I enquired if Maisey was working tonight and my face must have shown my disappointment when he replied with a simple, 'Nope'.

Things were to get worse when I asked where I might find her.

'You could try Tuona – it's the next town – but my guess would be that she's moved on.' When he had finished having his bit of fun he said, 'Sorry, young feller, she left on the noon stagecoach for Tuona, but she'll probably head further east.'

He probably tried to cheer me up by telling me about Meli, a young oriental girl who'd arrived on today's stagecoach and would be in later.

'Apparently these girls are trained to give a man pleasure,' the barman said and then advised me not to spread the word because I might have to join a queue. He whispered that the bank manager had already booked her at a special reserve price.

I finished my beer and told him that I was going to hit the sack because I was planning on leaving town early in the morning. I asked him to give Matt my apologies if he turned up.

THIRTEEN

I would have preferred Maisey's lovemaking to have sent me to sleep last night, but the beer had helped. I realize now that Maisey was right about it not being a good idea to see her again. She was an experienced woman and must have known many young fellers who thought they loved her.

I decided to give Larry's diner a miss as I strolled along Main Street heading for John's Livery and settled for picking up grub at the local store, something that I could chew on as I rode without needing to stop and cook something.

I'd reckoned that Matt would already be at work while most folks were still asleep so I was surprised to find the large wooden doors closed.

'Try around the back,' the white-haired man shouted from across the street.

I waved to him and took his advice and entered through the small back door. The inside was so dimly lit that I heard the groaning before I saw Matt curled up on the floor covered by a pile of blankets. His face was white as a newly washed sheet and he was obviously in pain.

'What's wrong, feller? You look all done in.' I said, and was taken aback when he replied in a weak voice that he'd been shot. I peeled back the blankets and saw the bloodstained dressing.

'A drink, I need some water,' he gasped, and pointed towards the water canteen hanging on a rail. I held the canteen to his lips and he sipped until it was almost empty. He started to tell me what had happened, but stopped and told me go and get some help and inform the marshal. He gripped my arm when he said that I best go to Tom the storekeeper and ask him to make sure he brought some stitching material and a bottle of whiskey. He even managed a smile when he said that Tom wasn't any good with animals, but was fine with bullet wounds. I made sure that he was in a comfortable position before I left. I hadn't noticed that Motty wasn't there.

Tom, the storekeeper, didn't react much to my news except to reach under the counter for a small black bag, grab a bottle of whiskey from the shelf and announce to his wife, Peggy, that he was off on some 'doctoring business'. Likewise, Marshal Johnson just grabbed his hat, frowned at his deputy and said that he had a good idea who had shot Matt. On the way to the livery he told me that Drew Simpson, Isobel's partner in crime and husband, had escaped from his cell last night. Simpson had offered to show the deputy some card tricks and the big dope had opened his cell. The marshal had returned from his late night rounds and found the deputy was locked in one of the cells and nursing a bruise on his thick skull. The marshal said he hadn't considered Simpson worth chasing after, seeing as how he hadn't committed anything really serious, not until now.

By the time we reached the livery, Tom, the storekeeper was laying out his instruments and shouted that he needed more light, so I opened the large front doors.

In between grimaces, Matt explained that the man jumped him while he was locking up last night, before making his way to join me for a drink During the struggle he shot Matt in the stomach and wouldn't help him, except for bringing him the materials to dress and bind the wound. At first light, the man had ridden off on Motty despite Matt telling him that horse was recovering from an injury. Matt described the man for Marshal Johnson which prompted the lawman to declare, 'That's Simpson all right. I'll get some help and then see if we can catch him, but he must have a good start by now. My guess is that he would have ridden out this end of town, rather than risk riding through Main Street.'

I asked to join the posse and the marshal said that I could borrow his spare horse. Before we left, Tom said that Matt would recover, but would have died during the night had it not been for the dressing he'd applied with that foul-smelling stuff. Matt even managed to joke that if it was good enough for the horses then it was good enough for him. Fifteen minutes later I rode out of town with the marshal and a posse of four others, including Ty Kylie, who had been on the trip to Indigo's yesterday.

When we reached the fork in the trail, the marshal signalled for us to pull up and then ordered me and Ty to follow the main trail while he and the others took the mountain trail towards Indigo's hideaway.

The marshal's sorrel gelding was more than a match for Ty's horse and we covered a lot of ground before we reached the hour limit that the marshal had set us before we were meant to turn back.

'There's a stagecoach station, not far from here,' said Ty, when I announced that our time was up. 'It can't be much more than a couple of miles, just beyond that pass we can see.'

I agreed that it would be worth riding to in case the folks at the station might have seen Simpson go by.

We were just leaving the narrow pass, and I was thinking that it must be a tight squeeze for the stagecoach, when I saw Motty standing by the side of the trail. He was holding his hoof off the ground, so it looked like the injury was still bothering him.

'That's my horse ahead,' I told Ty, and I was wondering where Simpson was, when he appeared from behind a rock, and he was pointing a pistol in our direction. It was the same man I'd seen talking to Isobel on the night we went to her room. He recognized me and said that if I tossed him my bankroll and let him have one of the horses then he'd let us live. I studied the face of the man with cold eyes and a heart to match. This was the man who was prepared to let a decent guy like Matt suffer a night of pain and the prospect of death without trying to help him.

The money wasn't important to me and not worth someone's life, but I could hardly trust Simpson. Perhaps I was too long in responding, or he just wanted to make sure I knew he meant business that caused him to shoot at Ty who fell from his horse and hit the ground with a sickening thud. I'd never fired a pistol from a sitting position before, but I managed to draw as Simpson trained his pistol on me. I didn't aim at any particular part of his body and was lucky that the bullet hadn't whizzed by him instead of entering his left eye. He was probably dead before he hit the ground, but I still kept him covered until I kicked his pistol out of his reach and checked that his evil doing was over forever. Luckily, Ty was only winded by the fall and had no more than a bullet wound in his arm, although it was bleeding quite heavily. I used his neckerchief to stem the flow of blood and tethered Motty to a gnarled cedar tree, having decided to take Ty to the stagecoach station.

The feller in charge of the station put a proper dressing on Ty's wound, but said he would need to see the doc when we got back to town. I'd told him about Simpson and he offered to send his son out and to take the body back to Dyers Gulch. He said something about having special funds for this sort of thing, but if there was room on the next stage-coach then the body could go up top with the luggage.

Ty was having trouble stopping himself from sniggering and on the way back to town he told me that he had an image of a trussed-up Simpson riding in the shotgun seat next to the driver. The same thought had crossed my mind.

The marshal was surprised when I told him to expect Simpson's body to be arriving in town later and he wanted to know every detail of what had happened. He asked what my plans were and I told him that I would check on Matt, buy me a horse and then head for home. I accepted the marshal's offer to let me buy the sorrel that he'd loaned me. As I shook hands with the marshal he said that I would make a fine lawman if ever I decided to wear a badge for a living. He would be pleased to show me the ropes if I came this way again and wanted to become a deputy. He knew about my search for Kelsall and warned me again not to take the law into my own hands.

'We need young men like you to keep our towns safe for the good folks,' he said. It was a different proposition to my grandpa's, but I knew that it would still involve killing.

Matt had been moved to a room above Tom's store so that he could be watched over while he recovered and I went there to say my farewell. I told Matt about what had happened to Simpson and I sensed that he was pleased. He was probably still hurting about his pa's killer never being brought to justice and might have felt it even more if his own attacker had got away.

I'd ridden slowly on the sorrel with Motty trotting alongside me and would have travelled through the night, had it not been for Motty's condition. The sky was clear and the full moon would have made the trail clear enough. I stopped near a small stream and picked myself a spot amongst some cedar trees to bed down for the night. I was to face the night wishing that I hadn't seen the partly decomposed faces of the little girl and her mother, which now kept reappearing. Most times when I tried to think of something else to take my mind off it, their faces would return and haunt me again. My mind was tortured and I could only hope that time would help, but until then I would have to try and live with it.

When I rose from my bed of rotten leaves I washed in the shallow stream nearby, while Motty and the sorrel slurped in the cold water. I gulped a few handfuls myself and we headed off on the final leg home. I wasn't looking forward to telling Grandpa about Jack. He'd known his fair share of grief, but he was bound to feel responsible for Jack's death because if he hadn't sent us off like he did, then Jack would still be alive.

FOURTEEN

When I saw the sign that read The Bryson Ranch I felt an almost boyish excitement. I was also relieved because for the past hour or so I'd had the uneasy feeling that I was being followed. I'd stopped a few times and hidden, hoping to catch whoever it was, but no one showed. Perhaps I was just being jumpy and maybe whoever shot me while I was fishing was a sick son of a bitch who took pot shots at strangers.

Grandpa could be a cantankerous old goat, but I'd missed his sense of humour and even the old tales he had a habit of repeating. I'd missed Trixie as well. No, she wasn't a girl; she was my dog, given to me by Grandpa on my thirteenth birthday along with my first pistol. She had been just a pup, but he told me that she would be a big dog on account of her being a husky/collie cross and because she had large paws. Trixie didn't grow like he'd said, but she was a beauty and as much Grandpa's favourite as mine.

It was early afternoon when I saw the ranch house and I urged the sorrel and Motty forward. There was smoke coming from the chimney and I spotted a few farm hands heading towards the cook-house. Grandpa was nearing his seventieth year, but he never seemed to slow down much so he might be out on the range, just keeping a guiding hand, as he put it. The place looked much just the same, except for two newcomers in the form of the Mexican-looking girl hanging out the washing near the house and the black and white dog that had come running towards us and was annoying Motty with his barking.

I hitched the horses to the rail at the front of the house and was brushing the trail dust from my clothes when I heard the front door open and I turned to greet Grandpa.

'What's your business here?' was the less than friendly greeting.

Joe Toomey my grandpa's foreman stepped down from the porch and looked puzzled before he said, 'Sorry, Sam. I didn't recognize you. What happened to that big black beast that no one else could ride?'

'Let's just say, I'm not very good at card playing. The guy who won it from me gave me Motty here. I think he did it out of pity, but he's a fine horse even though he doesn't look much. He's suffering from a cut on a front hoof, so I bought the sorrel to see me through the last leg home.'

I guessed Joe must have been just a bit more than forty years old. He was a loner, a mild-mannered, slim-built man, with light ginger hair. He'd never struck me as the sort to be involved in ranching, but he was trustworthy and firm with the hired hands.

The pup was tugging at my trouser leg and I laughed.

'I hope Trixie isn't jealous of this little rascal,' I said, and asked if she was with Grandpa.

'They're up on the hill, Sam.'

I looked towards the long hill that stretched away from the ranch house. I didn't suppose there'd been a day went by that Grandpa hadn't visited Grandma's grave up there.

I told Joe that I was going up there to surprise them and would have a talk with him later, but I was stopped in my tracks when he said, 'Your grandpa's dead, Sam, and so is Trixie. We buried them just over a week ago. I'm sorry.'

I don't know how long it was before I asked, 'How, was it an accident?' My question didn't seem right somehow. The truth was my mind was in a whirl. The news seemed unreal and it was as though I had just gone through the motions asking my question.

Joe hesitated before he answered. 'They were shot dead. It happened near your grandma's grave. Mr Bryson had gone up there to lay some fresh flowers and Trixie was with him. That's all we know. Chantico, the young housekeeper hanging out the washing over there, saw someone riding off.'

I asked if she could recognize them, but Joe said they were too far away and explained that her English wasn't very good and she seemed confused about what she saw. He'd asked the marshal to try and locate me and Jack, but they had no idea where I was or whether I was still alive.

'I hope you didn't mind me buying the new pup. Her name is Megan, which was chosen by the daughter of the man who sold it to me. I'll get rid of her if you'd rather buy one yourself to replace Trixie.'

I told him that we'd keep the pup. My thoughts were on other things, mainly what sort of scum would gun down an old man and his dog.

'Your grandpa's buried on the hill next to your grandma. I expect you'll want to go inside after your journey. I'll ask Chantico to prepare you some food and a drink. I've got to attend to a few things, but I'll drop by later and talk over some ranching matters. We've had a few problems with the stock and have missed your grandpa's experience.'

I asked him to send over Chantico so that I could speak to her, but told him that I didn't want anything else.

My talk with Chantico didn't help much. It was just like Joe had told me. She couldn't tell me anything useful, and was unable to describe the man she'd seen up on the hill or his horse. Chantico was obviously still upset by the event and kept wiping the tears from her eyes and repeating how Grandpa was a kind man. From what I could piece together she had been left homeless after her mother died. She and her little brother Emilio were thrown out of their home by a no-good rancher. She was concerned that she would be homeless again now that I was back and might not want them to stay. I told her not to worry. I didn't have the heart to tell her that I didn't really know what was going to happen to the ranch. Even at a sad time like this when my thoughts should have been elsewhere I couldn't help notice how pretty Chantico was. The inside of the house was just the same and I slumped into a chair and tried to take in the news. I suppose I'd always imagined Grandpa being sort of indestructible. I know it's stupid, but he was so full of life and had always been able to keep up with the hired hands during roundup. I could never remember him being sick and now he was gone.

I changed into a fresh set of clothes and discovered that the shirt was a little tight, reminding me that I had filled out a bit in the short time that I'd been away. Chantico gave me a shy smile when I passed her as I led the horses to the stables.

Jake, the stable lad, was a bit awkward as he tried to find the right words to tell me how sorry he was about Grandpa. I asked him to strip the saddles from both horses and give them a rub down and feed, warning him to be careful with Motty's injury. While I was saddling Grandpa's roan mare I asked Jake if he had any idea who might have killed Grandpa. I wasn't hopeful, but his reply didn't surprise me.

'Joe said that Coops and Dylan Cooper had been chased off the ranch by your grandpa a week before he died and he'd threatened to shoot them if he found them on his land again. Coops had been trying to make a move on young Chantico, but she wanted nothing to do with him.'

Jake hesitated before he replied when I asked him if he thought the Coopers were Grandpa's killers. 'They're a nasty pair, that's for sure. Dylan blinded a young cowhand with a broken bottle a few weeks back. Someone who saw it told me it was over nothing. He accused the kid of staring at his brother and the saloon girl he was groping. The kid said he was sorry if he'd caused any offence, but Dylan still did him with the bottle and laughed as the kid tried to find his way out of the saloon, screaming for help.' Jake paused and then sighed before adding, 'I wouldn't be surprised if they have killed someone, but I'm not sure they would risk killing your grandpa on his own land and so close to the house.'

I'd been hoping the Cooper brothers would have moved on by now or be locked away in some prison. They had always been bad news and I think they were one of the reasons Grandpa had some concerns about me being able to handle myself. They had tried to goad me into fighting them not long before I left to go after Kelsall, but I'd refused. I knew they wouldn't have let it go if I'd got the better of them. Grandpa had found out and hadn't hidden his disappointment in me.

Dylan Cooper had not been arrested over the attack on the cowboy he'd blinded because no one would dare testify against him and, according to Jake, the new marshal was dead scared of the brothers. I was puzzled why Joe hadn't mentioned the Cooper boys, but perhaps it was for my benefit, fearing that I might go after them.

I told Jake I was going into Chevin to speak to the marshal and he was to tell Joe where I'd gone when he got back.

I had only ridden the roan once before and was soon reminded how much livelier she was than even my old horse. She made Motty feel like a donkey and we soon covered the three miles to Chevin Falls.

110

The town was nothing special, except it had more than its share of nice people. Grandma had been a teacher at the school and we had attended the white wooden church on the edge of town every Sunday. The 'we' being Grandma and me. Grandpa usually managed to find some reason for not going, but on special occasions he wasn't allowed to get away with any of his long list of excuses. Grandma had given up on Jack when he'd reached the age of eighteen. She had hoped that if he ever married a good woman then his wife might persuade him to return to the fold.

A few of the folks strolling on the sidewalks greeted me as I rode along Main Street, but I could see the sadness and sympathy on their faces. Morgan Colby, who ran the local store, stopped sweeping outside his door and approached me. He wanted to make sure that I'd already heard the sad news, expressed his sympathy and then gave me a warning: 'I expect you've heard the rumours about the Cooper boys, but don't do anything silly, Sam. Those boys are as mean as hell and the new marshal is too frightened to even question them about your grandpa's death.'

I moved away from Colby's and heard Morgan shout after me, 'My Lucy has been looking out for you every day since you left.'

Lucy Colby was probably the prettiest girl in town, but we had spent too much time together

111

when we were kids. She had been like a sister to me, and always would be, I guess. I planned to talk to her soon and make sure that she understood that we didn't have a future together. I'd dropped hints, not wishing to hurt her feelings, but I'd have to make her understand for her own good.

The most obvious change on Main Street was the burnt-out shell of the Palace Saloon and the new addition of the Shelley's Heaven saloon opposite. I would find out later that the Cooper brothers were chief suspects for starting the fire, but no one would be prepared to testify that they had seen them running away from the burning saloon.

I soon discovered that my journey had been a waste of time because according to the slovenly looking deputy, the marshal was away visiting kinfolk for a few days. When I enquired about Grandpa's killing he replied in a dumb voice, 'I don't know anythin' about that 'cos I only arrived in town a few days ago. The marshal's my uncle and he's teachin' me the ropes, so to speak.' He told me his name was Lincoln Gosher, but folks called him Tubby.

I found out later that the old marshal, John Williams, had taken a job as a marshal in Stover County just before Grandpa was killed and his replacement was a newcomer who went by the name of Gideon Lombard. Marshal Williams had been a good lawman and well respected and it was a pity that he'd left. I just hoped the new marshal had more life in him than his nephew.

I rode the full length of Main Street before turning back and as I passed the saloon I was tempted to stop for a cool beer, but rode on. My dry throat would have to wait for refreshment because I couldn't risk meeting the Coopers, not until I'd spoken to the marshal.

I pushed the roan really hard on the way back to the ranch, angered by the thought of the Cooper brothers. I told Jake that I would take care of the unsaddling and I gave the animal a gentle rub down and lots of patting to help ease my conscience for pushing her so hard.

Chantico was waiting at the front of the house with a large jug of orange juice and a glass that was already filled. I gulped down the cool juice and had soon downed a second glass. I apologized for not offering her some and held the jug above one of the other glasses on the tray, but she declined, saying, 'No, thank you,' and lowered her soft brown eyes. There was a mixture of sadness and shyness about her and I suspected that her refusal was mainly because she felt it was wrong. It felt strange that a girl so close to my own age, as she was, might regard me as her superior.

I finished my third drink and trekked up the hill and knelt beside the graves of my grandparents.

I'd visited Grandma's before I left to go after Kelsall, but it hadn't been a sad time. I missed Grandma, but somehow memories of her had given me strength and even joy when I recalled many of the happy times and her funny ways. I knew it would be the same when I thought of Grandpa in the future, but for now I was just sad and I'm not ashamed to say there were tears on my cheeks.

It was nearing dark when I headed back to the house for supper and I was more confused and miserable than I had ever been in my life.

FIFTEEN

I was awake earlier than I wanted to be, but when I headed downstairs I discovered that Chantico was already in the house. She made me a giant sized breakfast that had me remembering Mick and his diner back in Bothey Waters.

My plans to ride out to the main cattle herd with Joe had to be delayed because of an unexpected caller. Mr Eli Beckstaff had been the family legal adviser for as long as I could remember. I watched him struggle to get down from his carnage and it crossed my mind that he could have been an undertaker, him being dressed in black from head to toe. There was no way of telling how tall the elderly man, with the sharp pointed nose and side-whiskers, might have been because of the severe bend in his back. I invited him into Grandpa's study and offered him a drink, but he declined and took a small bottle from his pocket, which he said was medicine. He swigged from the bottle like a cowboy who'd just returned from riding a dusty trail under the midday sun. He screwed the top on to the bottle and started a bout of coughing that seemed to go on and on before he finally spoke.

'I'm sorry for not making an appointment to see you, young Mr Bryson, but when I learned that you had returned I felt that we should meet as soon as possible in order to discuss some legal matters concerning your late grandfather's estate.'

He took a folder from his black case and handed it to me, explaining that one of the documents was a copy of the will. He had already offered his condolences, but repeated them again and then said he would summarize the will. He ended the summary by declaring that I was the sole beneficiary.

When I asked if there were any conditions, he started coughing again, but it didn't last long and he replied, 'There are no conditions and so the ranch is yours as well as any money held in the account specified. You will find a covering letter which you need to submit to the bank along with some form of identification.'

I asked if there was any provision made for my cousin Jack Bryson, then explained that Jack was dead.

'I'm sorry. I didn't know. Your cousin was to be allowed to remain living in the house he occupied for as long as he wished, but you were to remain the owner. There is a special clause which, now that you have returned, is somewhat academic. Your grandfather specified that if you had not returned home within a year of his death then everything was to be left to your cousin.'

Mr Beckstaff said that unless I had any questions that concluded his business, but he would be available at any time should I have a problem. All this legal stuff was new to me and I'm sure that some matters relating to the ranch would need attending to in the future. Grandpa had had more than his share of problems with land access and water rights in the past, as well as legal wrangles over the use of barbed wire to mark boundaries.

Mr Beckstaff halted as we walked to the door and reached inside his pocket and handed me a sealed envelope. He offered me a flustered apology and explained that my grandpa had deposited the letter with him only a few weeks before his death. Mr Beckstaff had been instructed to deliver it to me in the event of Grandpa dying before I returned.

After I'd waved him off, I sat on the steps of the porch and opened the envelope and read the following letter:

Sammy
I hope you never get to read this letter and that you

will have returned home and I will have told you all this to you face to face. Before I explain I just want to say that I have missed you, boy.

I was a stupid old man, picking on you like I did and sending you and your cousin Jack on that stupid test. So, I'm sorry for implying that you needed to prove that you had guts. I admired the way you stood up to me and now I pray that you have come to no harm.

Your cousin Jack is too wayward to ever run the ranch and I'll tell him when he returns that when the time comes I'll expect you to take over from me.

I just ask you to be yourself, always protect what is yours and defend the good name of the family. I have no doubt that you will do these things. Your grandma was always proud of you and so am I.

Your Grandpa
Albert Bryson

I returned to Grandpa's study, placed the letter in the top drawer of the desk and made a silent vow to my grandpa that I would find whoever had killed him and then I would track down Kelsall.

SIXTEEN

It was my third day home and I'd ridden out to look over the main herd with Joe Toomey. It felt strange as it sank in that this vast area of land was now mine. I told Joe about the will and thanked him for the help he was giving. He said that I could always rely on him and that was comforting to know. He mentioned that it would be quieter about the place without Cousin Jack, but looked troubled when he told me that he'd heard that Jack had spent a lot of time with the Coopers before we'd headed off after Kelsall.

When I asked Joe if he thought the Coopers might have been involved in Grandpa's death he paused for a while and then replied, 'If it was someone local who shot him then they would be top of my list, but proving it is another matter. I was sorry to hear about Jack and I wasn't suggesting he was like the Coopers. I suppose he just liked to live life to the full and the Coopers were always up for a good time.'

I made sure that I spoke to as many of the men as I could. I'd ridden with most of them, but there were some new faces, including a small group of Texans who had been hired since Grandpa's death.

I planned to ride into Chevin Falls tomorrow and talk to the new marshal. If the marshal wouldn't question the Cooper brothers, then I would.

When I approached the ranch house after stabling the roan on my return from riding out to the herd, Megan came scampering down the porch steps when she saw me and her tail was wagging like fury. I unbuckled my gunbelt and placed it on the rail just as Chantico and Emilio came out of the house. Chantico greeted me in her native language and then continued in rapid fire. I had told her that I could speak some Spanish and we had conversed a little, but Chantico had obviously forgotten that I could only manage a few words if they were spoken very slowly.

'Me,' I said, while jabbing a fmger in my chest and then added, 'no understand.'

'Chantico asked you if you wanted your dinner now,' Emilio explained.

I faced Chantico and spoke slowly in English. 'Later, thank you.' And then I asked the boy if he wanted to help me train the pup. He didn't answer my question, but just said that he liked Megan and threw the small ball that he'd been holding and laughed when Megan ran after it.

Emilio was a good kid and, unlike his sister, could speak English as well as his own language. Joe had told me that he was eight years old and was attending school. He was short for his age, but stocky and he had thick hair that was the colour of coal. He'd been a bit shy when I first tried talking to him the other day, but not anymore.

Megan was never going to be able to match the tricks that Trixie once did, but she was a lot of fun and sort of helped take my mind off things. I had seen a rider up on the hill twice since I'd been home and I had an uneasy feeling that it was either Kelsall or Grandpa's killer. I had been considering the possibility that Kelsall might have killed Grandpa!

SEVENTEEN

Within a couple of minutes of my first meeting with Marshal Lombard in his office I decided that all I'd been told about him was true and that he was in the wrong job. Unlike his nephew, Lombard was short and thin featured with small beady eyes that never stopped blinking. I wondered why he reminded me of Indigo's place and I guessed it was the rats that I'd seen in the shaft.

'So, you see, Mr Bryson, I can't act without any proof. Give me some solid evidence, perhaps a witness, then me and my nephew will have the Cooper brothers locked up and waiting for trial, and that's a promise.'

I suggested that he could at least question them and find out where they were on the day my grandpa was killed, but he said that he couldn't go hassling people just because they had a bad reputation. There was no chance of this man arresting the Coopers or anyone else and I was getting riled.

'Look, Marshal, if you're too spineless to do your job then you should give it up and I'll put myself forward to take your place. If you don't, then I'll complain to the town council and demand that they boot you out.'

His twitching and blinking increased and he tried to pacify me with some sympathetic remarks of how he'd heard that my grandpa was a fine man. He even tried to flatter me by saying that Grandpa would be proud of my determination to find his killer, but I wasn't interested in his bullshit and headed for the door.

'You could always become my deputy and then question the Coopers,' he shouted after me. His suggestion had me turning back and replying, 'I will if it gives me some authority and you let me do it my way and don't interfere.'

Tubby's mouth opened like a gasping fish when his uncle told him to give me his badge, promising to get him another one later. Tubby wrestled with the pin holding the badge to his food-stained shirt and ended up ripping it free.

The marshal took the badge out of his nephew's hand and was about to pass it to me when he said, 'I suppose I should make this formal and swear you in, but I've never done this before so I guess I'll just have to improvise.' He ordered Tubby to stand up and act as a witness and then asked me to raise my right hand and we had a sort of ceremony. He pinned the badge on to my shirt and stood back, looking pleased with himself when he said he needed to acquaint me with me a few things about the job. I told him that I didn't have time for all that because I was going to find the Coopers. I wasn't surprised when he made some excuse about needing to attend to some paperwork after I'd suggested that he come with me. I didn't extend the offer to Tubby who looked to be still sulking over the loss of his badge.

The atmosphere in the saloon was fairly lively and some of the familiar faces spotted the badge pinned to my shirt and they went into a huddled conversation. The barman was new and reminded me of the guy on the poster I'd seen in a store somewhere. It had been an advertisement for cut-throat razors. He looked about fifty, had black hair held down by grease and a large moustache that curled up at the ends. He would have looked more at home in a circus. When he poured me a beer he asked if I was new in town. I told him that I wasn't, but he must be if he didn't know me. I asked him if the Cooper brothers had been in the saloon today and I could sense folks looking in my direction. The barman claimed that he didn't know many of his customers by name, but I knew he was lying and so did the big feller at the end of the bar who was unsteady on his feet.

'He means Coops and Dylan,' the drunk slurred. 'The two no-goods who threatened to kill that feller last night unless he handed over the money they'd lost fair and square. Those evil bastards should be locked up.'

The big feller went back to staring down at his beer and the embarrassed barman said, 'Oh, those two. No, they haven't been in. They usually come in after the card games get under way and the girls start coming down.'

When he asked if there was going to be trouble I told him that there wouldn't be if the Coopers came quietly, but I guess everyone who heard me knew there would be.

I finished my beer and then headed for Doc Hanlon's small surgery, hoping he was there so that I could arrange for him to check over Motty. I remember him telling Grandpa once that a wound's a wound whether it's a man or an animal, makes no difference. Coming out of the doc's was the one person that I didn't want to see right now. It was Lucy Colby and she was holding a small kitten. Her face flushed when she said that she was planning to ride out to see me later and then babbled on a bit about how good I looked. She frowned when she saw the badge and asked why I'd become a deputy. I just said that I needed to try and help catch Grandpa's killer, but I didn't mention the Coopers.

'I expected you to have come calling on me by now, Sam. Pa said that you were in town the other day. Why didn't you come and see me then?'

I explained the best I could that I had a lot of things on my mind just now and that seemed to upset her some.

'So you can't find time to see me,' she said angrily, and would have said more, but I interrupted her.

'Lucy, we're never going to be more than good friends. I'm sorry. Most men would give their right arm to have you for their girlfriend, but we are too close, like brother and sister.'

She started to get hysterical and the tears flowed when she screamed, 'That's a horrible thing to say to a woman, and I am a woman, in case you haven't noticed.'

I tried to hug her, but she pulled away from me. I had my back to the street when a passing rider called out, 'You won't get anything from her, mister.' Then I heard the laughter, but I didn't turn around, still concerned that I had made a real mess of telling Lucy how I felt.

'Leave me be. I hate you,' she shouted, and then hurried away, but not before she had said, 'Perhaps one of those Cooper brothers would appreciate me in a way that you don't.'

I looked towards the two riders who had

laughed as they'd passed by without recognizing me. I watched them hitch their horses outside the saloon and then I opened the doc's door. Doc Hanlon peered over his small glasses and got up from his chair, held out his hand and said, 'Sam, welcome back, son. I'm real sorry about your grandpa. I'm a good listener if ever you want to discuss anything that's riling you or you want to chew over anything, outside of medical matters, I mean.'

Doc Hanlon was a small, rotund man with lively eyes that always seemed to be smiling when he wasn't talking about anything serious.

'It sounds as though your friend in Dyer's Gulch knew a thing or two about treating animals,' he said, after I'd told him about Motty's injury. 'I haven't got anything like his magic potion. He probably just needs to rest up and let nature take its course.'

I was glad that he hadn't mentioned Lucy because I was certain that like most folks he expected us to start real serious courting now that I was back. Anyway, I was sure the word would soon get out that whatever we were supposed to have had was now over.

I left the doc's and headed back to the saloon, without any particular plan except to try and keep calm. It would have been easier to have waited for the Coopers to ride into town and 'jump them',

but I wanted a witness in case things went wrong
and I ended up killing one or both of them. I
pushed open the swing doors and saw the brothers
standing at the bar and I was soon forgetting any
idea of staying calm. My instinct was to draw and
shoot them in the back, no warning, just gun them
down the way they'd done my grandpa. But something stopped me, telling me that it wasn't the way
to handle this. I headed to the left side of them,
not too close, but close enough to speak to them
without them being able to deliver a sly head butt.
The greasy-haired barman had signalled to them
with a nod of his head, making it clear to me that
he had already warned them that I was looking for
them.

Dylan was only about the height of most women
and I remember him being teased about it before
he started carrying a pistol. His black hair was
always greasy and dirty and he had most of his top
teeth missing. His eyes always reminded me of a
fish, being big and staring. Coops was a couple of
years of years older than Dylan, being about
twenty-five by my reckoning, and was a lot like his
brother except he was a mite taller. One of his fish
eyes was missing, not the result of fighting but of
some disease.

'I hear you want to speak to us, boy Deputy,'
Dylan sneered, and they both grinned. My voice
sounded nervous when I said I wanted them to

come to the marshal's office and answer some questions about my grandpa's death.

'Why would we want to do that?' said Coops, who grinned again and nudged his brother.

'Because he'd warned you to stay off Bryson land and you were seen up near our ranch house on the day some no-good coward killed him.'

'We might have been there to have another look at that pretty Mexican girl that your horny old grandpa wanted to keep to himself,' said Coops, and continued, 'Talking of girls, when are you going to give lovely Lucy what she's craving for, but pretends she isn't? Anyway, the old bastard couldn't have had much longer to live, so maybe we might have helped Mother Nature. He shouldn't have threatened us the way he did.'

My right hand tensed ready to draw, figuring that Coops had more or less confessed to killing Grandpa. Dylan tried to rile me more when he said that Coops would be happy to break Lucy in for me.

'I'm telling you to finish your drinks,' I said, my voice was calm and determined now, 'and come with me to the marshal's office. I'm not going to ask you again.'

'Now you're really frightening me, Deputy,' Coops mocked, and his brother added, 'We've seen you doing all that fancy shooting in the valley, but firing at an old coffee pot or bits of wood is kid's stuff. You best leave us in peace or your new job might end right here. Remember, even if you do get brave, there are two of us, and you ain't that fast. Anyway, we didn't kill the old feller.'

'You're lying vermin, now let's go,' I ordered, and braced myself, waiting for them to make the first move. They stopped sneering and turned to face me, their gun hands moving closer to their pistols. I saw some movement behind them as men scrambled to get out of the firing line and I heard men behind me taking the same precaution.

Dylan was the first to make a move towards his gun. I had a hunch that he might be the faster of the two and decided he was the one I would fire at first. My bullet thudded into his left shoulder, just where I intended. The impact sent Dylan sprawling backwards and knocked his brother off balance. I was within a hair's breadth of firing at Coops, but I didn't have to. Someone pointed at Coops and said, 'The dumb fool's shot himself in the foot.' Coops was hopping on one leg and crying like a baby. Only me and the sneaky barman were not sniggering or laughing, perhaps some were enjoying seeing the Coopers suffering and humiliated.

Dylan was doing a lot of muttering and groaning as he lay on the floor with blood dripping from his shoulder, causing a large red pool to slowly spread towards the bar.

I asked one of the men to go and get Doc Hanlon to come to the marshal's office and asked some others to help me get the brothers across the street and into the cells. I holstered my own gun and then picked up the Coopers' guns from the bar-room floor. When I ordered them to start heading for the marshal's office I was met with some protesting until I suggested that unless they wanted to bleed to death they needed to move quickly. Coops was struggling as he hopped on one leg until one man gave him a helping hand; another supported Dylan. I followed behind them, keeping both guns pointing at their back as they made their way across the street.

I wasn't sure whether Marshal Lombard was more shocked to see the blood on his office floor, or terrified at seeing the troublesome Coopers about to be jailed. He did manage an agitated, 'I thought you were going to ask them a few questions, not shoot them.'

I ignored his remark and suggested we placed them in separate cells to stop them trying to concoct a story before their trial.

Doc Hanlon arrived and said he hoped I wasn't going to be the sort of lawman who kept him busy, but he winked as he passed by and headed for the cells. It was nearly half an hour before he emerged carrying a small plate, containing the bullet he'd dug out of Dylan and the remains of Coop's big toe. Tubby started retching and headed outside. The doc shook his head and said the big feller might be off his food for a short while. Doc Hanlon suggested we let the brothers have any strong liquor they could afford, because they were in for a very painful time without it.

With luck the Coopers would stand trial and end up dangling on the end of a rope, but when I stepped outside the office I was greeted by a howling mob who wanted the brothers strung up right now.

Bob Stevens, an old friend of my grandpa was at the front of the mob and was carrying a rope. He appeared to be the ringleader and roared at me, 'Bring them out, Sam, or we'll burn them alive. They kicked my son senseless and now he can only sit in a chair all day, slobbering like a baby, unable to speak a single word or recognize me or his ma.'

'This isn't the way, Mr Stevens,' I shouted back. 'I'm sorry for your grief, but the law must take care of them.'

'We don't trust the law and nor should you. They killed your grandpa for God's sake.'

I saw flames flare up at the back of the crowd followed by shouts of, 'Burn the bastards!' I drew my pistol and fired into the air and then shouted for them to listen. The yelling stopped and I reminded them that if it wasn't for me the Coopers would be over in the saloon, waiting to commit their next act of violence or even killing. I appreciated that some of them had grievances, but I figured that I'd earned the right to say what happened, and I wanted them to have a trial. I ended by telling them to go home before some innocent men ended up dead. The silence continued for what seemed an age and then Bob Stevens shouted, 'Sam's right. It's his call.' A few others echoed their agreement and the mob slowly drifted away, leaving me to sigh and thank my lucky stars. I remembered Grandpa telling me that Marshal Williams had arrested the Coopers when Bob's son Charlie had been found in an alley, but there had been no one who had witnessed his beating. Charlie had made some sign to his pa that it was the Coopers, but he wasn't capable of repeating it in front of a jury.

Marshal Lombard appeared on the walkway once the trouble appeared to be over and I suggested that he and Tubby should make sure that the Coopers weren't left alone in case the trouble flared up again. He looked like a frightened rabbit as I left to head home.

A group of men were outside the saloon, but they seemed calm. I had just urged the roan to speed up, but pulled hard on the reins when I saw Doc Hanlon waving at me to grab my attention. He told me that he'd forgotten to tell me something really important and suggested we went into his office. What he told me was the biggest surprise of the day and left me wondering if I'd made a really big mistake.

EIGHTEEN

The events of the previous day caused me to ponder a few things over breakfast. Doc Hanlon's revelation was causing me real concern, but by the time I headed outside I was none the wiser as to what to do.

The sun was just rising and I hiked up the hill to the graves, more for something to do than to seek comfort by being near my loved ones. I sat by the graveside until I saw some activity down below, and when I headed down the hill the hired hands were riding off to start work.

Emilio came running towards me with the dog by his side and was excited when he asked if we could train Megan. He trudged away after I'd told him I was too busy, his head bowed in disappointment.

'Come on then, Emilio, let's teach your dog some new tricks,' I shouted after him. His mood changed in an instant as he ran back to me.

'You said my dog, is she my dog?' he asked, full of excitement.

'Well, she spends more time with you than me,' I replied and then added, 'so I guess she's yours.'

The boy ran after Megan with a hop and a jump as if Christmas had just arrived. And so it was back up the hill again for me, but soon after I had given Emilo some instructions of how to handle the dog he told me something that had me scurrying back down to the house. I had to work out a plan and I would need some help before confronting the man I now suspected was my grandpa's killer.

Within ten minutes I had saddled my horse and told Jake to tell Joe Toomey that I knew who had killed my grandpa and it wasn't the Coopers. Joe was to meet me at my cousin Jack's place where I would head after I'd been to town to make sure that no harm would come to the brothers, even though they didn't deserve much consideration. I had ridden a few miles from the ranch when I realized that I should have warned Chantico, but it was too late now.

Doc Hanlon didn't show much surprise when I told him what I had found out since our talk yesterday. He'd called to check on the Coopers earlier and discovered that Coops's foot had become infected and said that if he was a betting man then his money would be on Coops losing the foot before the week was out. I suggested that the brothers be moved for their own protection in case the mob got stirred up again, but the doc said that their condition was too bad for them to be moved.

I heard a guarded, 'Who is it?' when I banged on the marshal's office door. 'It's me,' I shouted back, and dopey Tubby opened the door, even though I'm sure he didn't know who 'me' was. The marshal and Tubby looked like they hadn't slept too much last night and the marshal's blinking was going at full speed.

'I hope you've come to relieve us,' said Marshal Lombard. 'I was just about to send Tubby to get Doc Hanlon because that feller Coops doesn't look too good. He can hardly speak and just keeps pointing at his foot.'

When I told them that the doc would likely amputate the foot, Tubby winced and asked, 'You mean cut his whole foot off?'

I nodded and the marshal looked towards the ceiling in reaction to Tubby's stupid question. The marshal had been told that it would take a couple of weeks to organize a judge for the trial. He got agitated when he told me that the town council wouldn't approve the expense of hiring extra deputies to guard the Coopers.

When I told him not to worry because there wasn't going to be a trial, at least not for the Coopers, he looked puzzled, and asked me if I'd changed my mind about letting the mob take care of them.

'I'm fairly certain that the Coopers didn't kill my grandpa and they need protecting from any mob. It would be best to move them from here, but Doc Hanlon advises that they should stay for now, because of their medical condition. Anyway, if Coops is going to have his foot sawn off then he'll definitely have to stay here.'

'So if they didn't do the killing, then who did?' the marshal asked.

'I'd rather not say, but you'll find out soon enough.'

'You seemed pretty certain about the Coopers,' the marshal said with a degree of sarcasm in his voice, which I guess I deserved. I told him that I was heading out of town now and hoped I'd be coming back with Grandpa's killer. I had mixed feelings about whether I wanted the killer to be spending tonight in the cells or in the offices of Herman Mason, the town's undertaker.

The ride up to Cousin Jack's place brought back memories of boyhood visits, but I hadn't been there for a long time. I guided my horse away from the shale-covered path that led towards the small log cabin. I'd always avoided shale since some had pierced the hoof of a previous horse, but that was nothing compared to Motty's recent injury.

I checked around the back and then entered the house, having first drawn my pistol. Judging by the general state of the house it looked as though Jack hadn't bothered with housekeeping. I checked my timepiece and decided to wait for half an hour, sitting myself out on the porch so that I could see any approaching rider. I became impatient after the twenty minutes and headed back home, thinking that I might meet the killer on the way.

My intention to go to the stables and ask Jake if Joe Toomey had checked in was put on hold when I saw a distraught Chantico rushing towards me. I was having more difficulty than usual trying to understand her, but I finally picked up enough to figure out that she'd seen a man riding off with Emilio.

'Do you know the man?' I asked, eager to get after him.

She shook her head and said, 'Too far to see,' and pointed in the direction I'd just come from. I could have asked her how long ago, but it would have been wasting time. I climbed up on to the roan while it was on the move and it was soon into a full gallop, but I feared it was a lost cause. If the kidnapper had ridden this way he must either have a head start, or had taken cover somewhere, otherwise we would have met on the way back from Jack's.

When I reached the trail that led up to Jack's place for the second time that day I pulled up the roan. The killer's horse was tied to the hitch rail meaning that he wanted me to come here again. I was riding into some sort of trap as I went slowly towards the house, but I had no choice. I was jumpy, because I'd never been in this position before, waiting to be shot at from close range. I edged towards the cabin knowing that I was an easy target, thinking that my only hope would be that his aim was poor. The hitch rail was in touching distance when the door opened and I saw the terrified face of Emilio, clutching his puppy. He was being restrained by the left arm of Joe Toomey, who was pointing Grandpa's pistol at me. Grandpa had had the pistol specially fashioned to his own design and was the only one of its kind in the world according to the gunsmith who had made it. The most notable features were the extra long barrel and the Bryson brand on the handle. Grandpa hadn't ever been the sort to pose or show off and I'd always been puzzled why he'd bought the gun because he never wore it. I don't think he'd ever bothered to fire it. I did handle it once and remember thinking it wasn't the sort of gun I would want if I was in a tight spot.

'Dismount as slowly as you can,' Toomey ordered, and then threatened me by saying, 'I've told this kid that I'll shoot him and his yappy dog if he makes a wrong move. He's a smart kid and he knows I mean it and you'd better as well.'

'Why, Joe? Why did you shoot Grandpa? Was it because he found out that you had been robbing him?'

'Who told you that?' he snarled, showing an aggression that I had never seen before.

'Doc Hanlon said that Grandpa told him that he was going to boot you out, but that was some weeks before he was killed. The doc thought that Grandpa must have changed his mind, perhaps because he treated you like a son.'

'That's rich. Anyway, I only took what's rightfully mine,' Toomey snarled and then added, 'I even offered to share the ranch with you, but the old swine would have none of it.'

'Why would he want to do that?' I asked, puzzled by his remark. Toomey had worked hard for Grandpa, but he'd been well paid.

Toomey said, 'Because he was my pa, that's why.'

I was dumbstruck. Toomey was a bit older than what my pa would have been, but Pa only had one brother and that was Uncle Saul, Cousin Jack's dad, and he was dead. I didn't want to rile Toomey, in case he became even more agitated as he held on to Emilio, so I kept quiet.

'He accused my own ma of being a whore and said I could have been fathered by any one of a hundred or more. I'm not denying that she liked men, but she wasn't like he said.'

'Perhaps he thought you were trying to trick him in some way,' I suggested, and added, 'He was a fair man. You know that!'

'Not over this he wasn't, and that's why I killed him. He shouldn't have blackened my ma's memory. She had kept quiet all those years to protect your family and only told me after your own grandma had died.'

I tried to control my anger for the sake of Emilio. I had never hated anyone more than the cowardly good-for-nothing who had just confessed to killing Grandpa.

Emilio must have tensed when he heard Toomey repeat his threats and squeezed Megan, who yelped and then wriggled free. In the commotion, Emilio somehow broke away from Toomey. I quietly cursed myself because I hadn't drawn my gun during the distraction. Toomey didn't bother to grab Emilio again, and I soon realized why when Toomey spoke.

'You really are dumb coming after me. You must have known that I'd kill you. Perhaps you thought I would let the kid go. I'd like to, but I can't, because I have a plan. With you, the kid and his sister dead I can say you decided to run off with them, leaving me in charge. That way I as good as get my inheritance after all.'

'What about Jake? He knows that I was after

you,' I said, hoping that my bluff would unsettle him.

Toomey smiled. It was surprising how different he looked from the man I'd known for years. He had been acting a part until today and now I was seeing the real Joe Toomey.

'Jake probably hated your grandpa more than I did after the way he was always on the kid's back. And he probably hates you at the moment because he thinks you've spoilt his chances with Chantico. Not that it matters, because you've signed Jake's death warrant, because he'll have to go 'missing'. Or maybe I could say he was lusting after Chantico and you killed him in a jealous rage and that would explain why you'd run away with the girl and the kid. Yeah, I like that idea. I'll suggest to the marshal that you've fled to Mexico. But I might just have a little fun with the girl before I kill her. She's a bit too sweet for my tastes, but she's all woman with those child-bearing hips of hers. Yes, I just might have her. She'll scratch and scream, of course, but it won't matter none. She might even end up enjoying it like some of the others have.'

My hand was itching to draw my pistol as I felt the hatred for this man rise inside me. I told him he was a sick son of a bitch and that I'd kill him right now if the boy hadn't been in danger.

Toomey laughed. 'I know you're fast, kid, but remember I've got this big beauty pointing at you.

Anyway, I don't think you've got the stomach for killing, otherwise you would have killed the Coopers when you thought they'd shot your grandpa.'

I was on the point of trying to catch him by surprise, when the dog tugged at the legs of his pants. It gave me the chance I'd been waiting for, but he'd recovered and was pointing the gun in my direction when my own gun reached the firing position. The bullet entered his forehead and ended his miserable life before he managed to pull the trigger, but it was fired by someone from behind me. I rushed forward and kicked his gun away and then pulled the sobbing Emilio to one side, preventing him from seeing the twisted features of Toomey's face. I scanned the area from where the shot that had saved my life must have come from and decided that it had been fired from the shelter of the trees. I didn't feel that I could be in any danger from Toomey's killer as I figured he would have fired at me by now. I climbed up on to the roan and told Emilio to hold on to the dog with one hand and then I pulled him up.

Emilio was still sobbing when we approached the trees and I saw the rider coming towards us. He was holding a rifle in one hand and his reins in the other. I lowered Emilio to the ground and told him to run and hide amongst the trees. I promised him that he wouldn't come to any harm.

I was about to ask the rider if he'd fired the shot and what his business was here which might have seemed pretty odd given that he'd just saved my life. It was hard to put an age on the man because he had a heavy beard and looked as though he had been sleeping rough. I watched him carefully in case he raised his rifle.

'Sam, it's me, Cousin Jack,' he shouted, and laughed as he dismounted and then pushed the rifle into the scabbard that was strapped to his horse. I should have recognized his grey gelding, but I had been distracted by what happened with Toomey.

I dismounted and shouted for Emilo to come out as I approached Jack and we shook hands. When we hugged I was left in no doubt that Jack had been sleeping rough when the smell of his soiled clothes and sweaty body hit my nostrils.

Jack looked strained and although he was a Bryson he must have favoured his ma's side being short and squat. His fair hair was greasy and scruffy under the badly stained Stetson that came close to covering his eyes.

I was stunned when it sank in that it really was Jack.

'Jack, I thought you were dead. I saw a body back in Klanbala and I arranged to have it buried in your name. I was convinced that you'd been killed by Sharkey Kelsall. Did you ever catch up with him?'

Jack shook his head. 'I was on my way to Klanbala when I developed some sort of fever. I was looked after by an old couple and when I got better I had bad luck at cards and I've been living rough as I made my way back. I was going to tell Grandpa that I wasn't interested in the ranch, but it's too late now. Jake told me about Grandpa's death and how you suspected Toomey. I figured that you might have headed this way and decided it was worth riding by.'

'Lucky for us that you did,' I said.

'Is the kid all right?' he asked, showing some real concern.

'He's back there and he's fine. Let's go and take him home.'

I shouted for Emilio to come out and when he appeared he had stopped sobbing but he still looked nervous.

'Hi, little buddy,' Jack called out.

I asked Jack to lift Emilio and the dog on to my horse and suggested that he rode home with us to have some grub, but he declined and surprised me when he said with a smile, 'I wouldn't want to spoil your welcome when that Mexican girl sees that her brother is safe. She sure is a pretty one. I only spoke to her for a few minutes, but she was just as concerned about you as she was for her brother. I reckon that girl is sweet on you – big time sweet, I would say.'

'What does big time mean?' Emilio asked. 'I know Chantico likes Sam. Is that what big time means?' I laughed with Jack and he told Emilio that it did.

'Before you go, Sam, I have to ask you something. Why did you suspect that Toomey was Grandpa's killer?'

'It was Emilio here who helped me. I knew Toomey wasn't quite what he seemed when I discovered that he'd been fiddling the books and pocketing some money, but never figured that he'd harm Grandpa.'

'So how did Marshal Emilio help?' Jack asked, and Emilio giggled.

I explained that while I was helping Emilio train Megan we saw Toomey go by and Emilio said that we must keep Megan away from him because Toomey had kicked Trixie after she bit him while he was arguing with Grandpa up near the grave.

'Did he actually see the shooting?' Jack asked.

'No. He wasn't supposed to be playing where he was and had been hiding in some bushes. He had come down the hill and heard the shots but had been too scared to say anything. Toomey had told me that he was out on the range on the day of the killing so I decided to flush him out with the help of Jake.'

I told Jack that I would report Toomey's death to the marshal and explain how it happened. I would arrange for Toomey to be buried and that I would call on him tomorrow about noon. When I said that I hoped he'd come back and work on the ranch, he just said, 'I'm not sure that would be a good idea, Sam, and in any case I have plans of my own. I'll be moving on soon.' He ruffled Emilio's hair and led his horse away in the direction of the cabin.

The marshal didn't seem interested in what had happened to Toomey and said that seeing how I vouched for Jack there was no need for the law to get involved.

Doc Hanlon wanted to know all the details and he approved of my idea of involving Jack in the running of the ranch and thought we would make a great team once we got some experience. He was so fired up with the idea that I didn't have the heart to tell him that I was beginning to have my doubts because I had plans that didn't involve ranching. Before I left town I called on Herman Mason the town's undertaker and arranged for the burial of Toomey for tomorrow. He was a slightly built man with an extra large nose that had a distinctive bend in it. The story goes that his nose was broken when he fell on to a coffin as it was being lowered into the ground. He didn't strike me as the sort to get involved in brawling so maybe the story was true.

Mr Mason looked a mite surprised when I said that no one from the ranch, including myself, would be present at the burial.

'But I thought he was. . . .' The undertaker didn't finish his question, perhaps reminding himself that it would be out of place. He assured me that everything would be attended to.

NINETEEN

I was finishing my breakfast when Chantico came in and apologized for not being there earlier to serve me.

'It's my fault for being up before the birds,' I said, but she seemed upset and I added, 'I have things to take care of before I go and meet my cousin Jack at noon. I plan to bring Jack back with me for a sort of celebration, so perhaps you could prepare something special for us.'

Chantico seemed pleased that she could do something to help and told me not to worry about Emilo who had settled down last night and hadn't suffered from yesterday's experience.

I'd come to a decision about what I wanted to do, but I needed to talk things over with some of the men and then it would depend on how my meeting with Jack went.

The sun was already as hot as hell by the time I

rode off to where the main herd was grazing and where I would find Cornelius Clayton, the man I had made the new foreman. Clayton didn't have the experience of Toomey, but I had a hunch that he would handle the job well and he had the respect of the men.

When I reached the area we call High Ridge I saw Clayton supervising some of the hands who were mending a damaged fence. He peeled off his gloves and came to greet me. Clayton was close to fifty, tall and lean and had a severe limp, the result of a bullet that was still lodged in his knee, but he never complained about the pain that it must cause from time to time. Grandpa had told me that Doc Hanlon was surprised that Clayton could walk at all. He'd tried to dig the bullet out, but decided it was too risky. At least Clayton had the consolation of knowing that the cattle rustler who fired the bullet was shot dead. I'd just remembered that it happened right here on High Ridge a couple of years ago.

My meeting with Clayton had gone well and he had seemed pleased with my ideas for the ranch. Now I just needed to sell the idea to Jack. He would need to be persuaded because he wasn't the sort who liked responsibility. He was a free spirit, I suppose. As I rode towards Jack's cabin my thoughts were on yesterday and I wondered if

Toomey's body was already in the ground of the town's cemetery. If it hadn't have been for Jack then it might have been the day of my funeral. My thoughts of funerals were disrupted by gunfire that must have come from behind the rocks at the side of the trail. The single shot caused the roan to stop and rear up and I was thrown to the ground with a thud, leaving me dazed and at the mercy of whoever had fired the shot. By the time I had recovered after taking shelter, the bushwhacker must have fled, because when I searched behind the rocks he had gone.

It took me a few minutes to calm the roan and he still seemed spooked when I settled into the saddle and then nudged him to continue my ride to Jack's place which was close by. It wasn't only the roan that was jumpy and I was glad when I saw Jack's cabin ahead.

Perhaps Jack's shot at Toomey yesterday was just a fluke because his eyesight wasn't too good. He came out of his cabin and was pointing a rifle at me.

I laughed as I dismounted and said, 'Howdy, Cousin, can't you tell a friend from a foe?' But Jack wasn't smiling when he yelled back, 'Hold it right there, Sam.'

'What's this about, Jack?'

'It's about one of us dying here right now and the other owning the ranch, Sam. It's that simple.'

'But that's why I'm here, Jack. I've come to tell you that you can run the ranch with Cornelius Clayton. You'll be in charge because I'll be leaving.'

Jack laughed and said, 'I don't want to run the stinking ranch. I plan to sell it and then leave this hellhole and see a bit of real action. Do myself a bit of gambling; surround myself with some pretty women. That's what I want, but I'm going to give you a chance, Sam. Maybe all that practising you used to do might just save you.'

'Why did you save me yesterday, Jack, if you planned this?'

'I'd planned to kill Toomey and I took my chance yesterday. I didn't do it for you. Toomey told me that he was my uncle and he just wanted to do right by us. He didn't say anything about killing Grandpa, just that he'd make sure that we'd both have a stake in the ranch after we'd taken care of you. When Grandpa sent us after Kelsall, Toomey told me to make sure that you didn't come back. So I trailed you and not Kelsall. It was me who shot you while you were fishing on your way to Bothey Waters. I was sure that you were dead and I was on my way home when I developed the fever and nearly died. That's why I look like shit. It was one hell of a surprise when I found out that you were still alive and if that kid hadn't been here yesterday I would have finished you off then.'

'You needn't do this, Jack. You haven't done any

real harm. Toomey deserved to die and we can forget about the threats you've made here. So let's talk this over.'

'There's something else you don't know, Sam. It was me who killed Tommy. Kelsall had already set off for who knows where when me and Tommy carried on playing cards. We got into an argument and I shot him. I told your grandpa that I'd seen Kelsall ride off and then I found Tommy dead. You didn't say yesterday, but I take it you never got close to finding Kelsall?'

I just shook my head. I was thinking that I might have killed an innocent man if I had caught up with him.

'What made you turn bad, Jack?' I asked, and then added, 'Grandpa was good to you.'

'You were always the favourite, Sam. Sure he treated me OK, but I was never your equal, not even in Grandma's eyes.'

I could see the hurt in his face, but for a moment I thought he might be having second thoughts about killing me as we talked about family, but his face hardened as he dropped the rifle to the ground.

'The talking is over, Sam. I think Grandpa was right about you being a yella belly and now you're going to die without ever knowing what it's like to kill a man. All that fast-draw shit means nothing now.'

I could have told Jack he was wrong as he went for his pearled handled Colt. My first shot hit him between the eyes and the second thudded into his body. I'll never forget the look on his face as he fell to the ground, dropping his pistol before he fell on to his back. It only needed a glance at Jack's eyes staring to the sky to realize that I now had no living kin left. At least none that I knew of.

I didn't suppose I would ever know whether Toomey's claim that he was Grandpa's son was true, but I had already decided that I would let it die with him and I wouldn't mention it to anyone. I would tell the marshal that Jack had pulled a gun on me, intending to kill me to inherit the ranch, but I didn't expect Lombard to be interested in any of it.

I dragged Jack's body into the shade and covered it with the blanket I got from inside the cabin. Jack had been a fool, and despite the smile and carefree nature he must have been bitter inside and just as bad as Toomey.

I rode the roan hard on the way back to the ranch, knowing that it wasn't Jack who had shot at me earlier and whoever it was might be out there ready to try again. I don't know why, but I had a feeling that it wasn't Kelsall.

TWENTY

It's the second time this week that I've come up here to visit the graves because I have some serious thinking to do. It always seems to help being here. Cousin Jack is buried next to Toomey in the town cemetery because he didn't deserve to be buried here with loving kin.

Life's been good to me since I first visited Grandpa's grave almost twelve years ago, but the scene below doesn't look much different as I look down. I can see a dog, but it isn't Megan, although Laddie, our latest dog, looks a lot like her. Megan didn't get to make old bones and died a couple of years ago. There are a few others who are no longer with us, like Doc Hanlon and Mr Beckstaff. Joshua Beckstaff looks after the legal stuff and one day he'll look the spitting image of his pa, Eli. I just hope he gets to keep a straight back. The Cooper boys are dead. A few weeks after they left the cells,

156

with Coops still hobbling on both feet, they got into an argument and Coops killed Dylan. Coops was so cut up about what he'd done that he shot himself the following day, but this time he meant to and he died.

I can see the boys playing near the stables and one of them looks just like his ma and is about the same age as Emilio was when I first saw him. His name is Raoul and he looks like Emilio did with his coal-coloured hair. The other boy is Samuel, and he's a year older than Raoul. In case you're wondering, Emilo is back East and training to be a lawyer.

I often reflect on the day I killed Cousin Jack and wonder what made me decide to be a lawman. It just seemed right, I guess, and that's why I put Cornelius Clayton in charge of the ranch and returned to Dyer's Gulch and became Seth Johnson's deputy. Within two years I was marshal, but Seth still gave me a guiding hand and even advised me how to handle my wife who has never been pleased at my decision to become a lawman.

I can see another face from the past arriving. It's the man who took a shot at me when I was on my way to see Cousin Jack and he's now my best buddy. It's Jake and his wife is with him. He's still the stable lad, except he isn't a lad any more and he's piled on the beef since he married and moved into Jack's old place. Jake confessed to me a few days after he shot at me that he'd wanted to try and frighten me into leaving the ranch, fearing that I might 'steal' the girl he was now married to. He feels as guilty as hell about it, but at least his confession meant I wasn't looking over my shoulder all the time. Some folks might find it strange that I became the best of buddies with a man who fired at me from those rocks, but Jake is not that bad a shot and I know that he meant me no harm. I never did hear what happened to Sharkey Kelsall, or discover the identity of the man that I arranged to bury in the Klanbala Town cemetery thinking it was Jack. Maybe Kelsall sold his horse to the dead man and Grindley shot him. I hope that's what happened because Grindley was hanged for murder, even though the records will show that Jack Bryson was the victim.

Chevin Falls has changed some since the railroad came to us a couple of years ago and that was part of the reason why I took the marshal's job at the same time and I have helped make it one of the safest towns in the territory. But in recent months the ranch has been plagued by rustlers and illegal grazing and ranch hands have been threatened.

I start my walk down the hill, wondering if I had made the right decision to hand in my marshal's badge so I can protect the ranch from those who have no respect for the law. I have tried doing it the legal way, but from tomorrow I won't be hampered by the badge.

When I reach the ladies they stop chattering long enough for me to kiss them and Chantico goes inside to make us all a drink. I know it's all a mite confusing but Jake is married to Chantico.

I will always have reason to cherish the seventh gun in my collection which is the Remington Frontier that I bought to replace the same model that I'd used when I shot my cousin Jack. I bought it at Colby's store and it was there I met Lucy Colby again. Maybe it was that pretty blouse she was wearing that made me realize that I didn't see her as a sister any more.

I'm not proud to say that I have killed thirteen men, mostly in the line of duty, so I guess that Grandpa and Cousin Jack had both misjudged me. But Grandpa was right that the law could only protect a man's property and rights up to a point. I've discovered that and from tomorrow some no-goods are going to be in for a hell of a surprise when I tackle them without wearing a badge. From tomorrow I will do it Grandpa's way, but I will never allow my gun to belong to Satan.